Hell

Yasutaka Tsutsui

Translated by Evan Emswiler

ALMA BOOKS

ALMA BOOKS LTD
London House
243–253 Lower Mortlake Road
Richmond
Surrey TW9 2LL
United Kingdom
www.almabooks.com

First published by Alma Books Ltd in 2007
This paperback edition first published in 2008
Original title: *Heru* (*Hell*)
Copyright © Yasutaka Tsutsui, 2003
Originally published in Japan by Bungei Shunju Ltd. Tokyo.
English translation © Evan Emswiler 2007
All rights reserved.

*This book has been selected by the Japanese Literature Publishing Project (JLPP),
which is run by the Japanese Literature Publishing and Promotion Center (J-Lit
Center) on behalf of the Agency for Cultural Affairs of Japan.*

Yasutaka Tsutsui and Evan Emswiler assert their moral right to be identified
as the author and translator of this work in accordance with the Copyright,
Designs and Patents Act 1988

Printed in Great Britain by CPI Cox & Wyman, Reading, RG1 8EX

ISBN-13: 978-1-84688-046-9

HELL

It was late in the afternoon, and Nobuteru was rough-housing with two friends up on the school-yard platform used by the teachers to address the student body. It was five feet above the ground and a bad fall could have been dangerous, but this was far from their minds. Boys their age are confident that they'll never be the ones to get hurt. Besides, it wasn't the first time they played this game, and falling had always meant nothing more than cuts and bruises. They were covered in sweat and dirt and dressed in little more than rags, since new clothes could only be bought with war-ration coupons. They must have smelt awful, but they didn't notice; boys in the fourth year of primary school never think about hygiene. Their only concern was knocking each other off the platform.

Yuzo, the biggest and most boisterous of the three, laughed loudly, revealing missing front teeth. He wiped his nose, smearing a slimy trail of snot onto his palm, which he stuck in Nobuteru's face.

Nobuteru screeched and leapt back – crashing into Takeshi behind him. Takeshi lost his footing and went tumbling off the platform. He landed on the ground awkwardly, body askew, and immediately began to wail. He was hollering something about his leg. From the way Takeshi was moaning, Nobuteru should have known this was no ordinary injury, but this realization would only come to him much later and with a great deal of guilt as he replayed the moment in his mind. Instead, Yuzo and Nobuteru exchanged embarrassed grins, jumped to the ground, and grabbed Takeshi's left ankle. They began to pull him around by his oddly bent leg, singing, "Don't cry, my little dove! You'll always be my one true love!" They were trying to stop his tears by making him laugh.

But Takeshi's leg was broken. His cries grew louder and soon the teachers came running. He was quickly loaded onto a stretcher and driven to the hospital in the small truck that delivered the school lunches.

When he finally returned to school, he was on crutches, and the leg never mended completely.

From that point on, Nobuteru couldn't bring himself to talk to Takeshi or even look him in his timid face.

But wait, there was something strange about this. They couldn't possibly have sung 'Don't Cry, My Little Dove'. The song didn't exist until after the war. Could Nobuteru have added this detail later in life? Still, he couldn't for the life of him think what other song they might have sung that day.

Not long after this incident, just before he became a fifth-year student at school, Nobuteru and his family moved to Sasayama in Hyogo Prefecture. Students without relatives in rural areas were evacuated as a group soon after, but Nobuteru had no idea what happened to Yuzo or Takeshi. When the war was over, Nobuteru and his family returned to the city. Their house had escaped damage, but the houses of most of his friends were levelled in the air raids. Neither Takeshi nor Yuzo ever returned to school.

* * *

"Motoyama's a yakuza now, you know."

Nobuteru had just entered college when a classmate from primary school told him this. It wasn't much of a surprise that Yuzo, with his bad grades and wild disposition, would become a gangster. But Nobuteru had fond memories of the times they spent together (with the exception of the accident that crippled Takeshi), and he had even come to think of Yuzo, the boy with missing front teeth, as his best childhood friend.

Nobuteru was seventy years old. He had done many bad and foolish things in his life; he was probably no better than Yuzo in that respect. For a while his pursuits had even skirted the underworld that Yuzo inhabited, and he had often mused about being reunited with his old friend one day. But at his primary-school reunion just after he had turned fifty, he learnt that Yuzo was killed in a gang fight while in his twenties. Nobuteru was shocked. All this time he had been reminiscing about a friend who had been dead for decades. How could Yuzo be dead while Nobuteru still lived?

Nobuteru himself had come close to death many times, although not in any way similar to the way Yuzo died. And at his advanced age, Nobuteru had another brush with death – in a way that seemed the domain of Japan's elderly. Alone at home on New Year's Day, he decided to add a *mochi* rice cake to the leftover soup. He remembered growing up hungry when food was scarce, and he loved the *mochi* that he had been deprived of as a child. He was slurping the soup like a greedy monkey, savouring every last bit of flavour, when the gooey mass of *mochi* got lodged in his throat. Suddenly he couldn't breathe. He poked a finger in his mouth to hook the *mochi* out, but succeeded only in poking it further down his throat. He fell to the floor, gasping, his mind growing dim. He was reaching the point of no return. But he'd be a laughing stock, dying like this! Finally, he yanked out his dentures. The *mochi* stuck to the false teeth and slithered back up his throat as he pulled them out of his mouth.

How many times had he managed to cheat death? And how many more times would he do so before the end finally came? If he were younger, he might have rejoiced at having survived, but age had changed him. He was tired. Now something as insignificant as the way young people spoke was enough to set him off. He hated how they would say they "could care less" when they meant that they "couldn't care less". "You got a mobile, man?" they would say. What was that supposed to mean? But as a boy, Nobuteru's conversations with Yuzo had been peppered with slang like "nif-tee" and "slick", and as a college student he was known to refer to more than one girl as a "fox".

Yuzo died after entering an enemy gang's territory with two subordinates in tow. He was courageous almost to the point of foolishness, but he had no idea that he was walking to his death, and neither did Daté, who was right behind him. Daté was nineteen and in awe of Yuzo.

It was eight o'clock on an autumn night. Daté was walking cockily with his shoulders thrust back, just like Yuzo. He and Hattori, another protégé of Yuzo's, walked together behind Yuzo through a back alley of the Misugi shopping arcade – a red-light district of bars, tiny restaurants, *yakiniku* barbecue joints and establishments of questionable repute. It was the Ikaruga gang's territory, and that meant trouble for members of any other gang, but Daté had no fear of death. Yuzo seemed invincible to him, and as long as Daté was with Yuzo, death held no sway over him.

Yuzo turned back at Daté and grinned. "Hey, Weasel. You're not gunnin' for my job, are you?" Weasel was Daté's nickname.

"Who, me? I'm just a weasel." It was one of Daté's running jokes.

Hattori smiled at the two of them.

The camaraderie of the three men came to an abrupt end moments later when Yuzo was stabbed in the gut. Four members of the Ikaruga gang appeared, surrounding Yuzo, and after a brief shouting match they attacked him. But it was hardly a gang fight, as Nobuteru's classmate had called it. The men who killed Yuzo didn't even know that he belonged to the Sakaki gang. Yuzo fell to the ground as if bowing down before his attackers, and Daté's illusions crumbled with him. How could Yuzo be killed so easily?

Daté and Hattori had been walking a bit behind Yuzo, and stopped in their tracks when the trouble started. The Ikaruga gangsters didn't even realize that the three men were together. But then Hattori turned and ran, drawing their attention towards him. Daté also turned and made a haphazard dash for the main shopping strip, pushing people out of his way. He felt like he had walked out onto the balcony of a high-rise apartment only to find that he had stepped out of a window instead.

Hattori had turned right onto the main street, so Daté turned left. He was grateful that fear hadn't rooted him to the spot; at least he was running. He ran and ran, giving silent thanks with every step. But he felt his knees grow weak as he heard the footsteps of his pursuers behind him.

"They're gonna kill me," he said to himself matter-of-factly. "I'm gonna die."

He turned again into a back alley, nearly getting tripped up by a plastic bucket before colliding with someone. He felt like he was already dead. His stomach felt pumped full of air and about to pop out of his throat. His guts were churning.

He stumbled into a narrow alley lined with the back entrances to shops. If he wasn't careful, he'd get trapped. He ran into another side street, panting, a desperate wheeze leaking from the back of his throat. Could that dark figure ahead be one of the gangsters? He doubled back, but no matter how far he ran, he never came out onto a main road. It was one back alley and narrow side street after another. It was just a matter of time before they got to him and put an end to his short life. If only he could go home and crawl into bed!

Daté pissed his pants as he ran. The warmth of his urine excited him, and at the same time it heightened his fear. He began to tremble. Death was close. Something approaching adoration came over his face as the surprisingly sweet scent of death filled his nostrils. And still he kept running, and running, and running.

Thinking about Takeshi always left Nobuteru consumed with guilt, and so he did his best to avoid it. When he heard that Takeshi had graduated with honours from a prestigious university and was working his way up the ranks of a large corporation, he felt an odd mixture of pain and relief, but he couldn't shake a certain uneasiness. Even in his success, Takeshi could not have forgotten what Yuzo and he had done to him. Takeshi and Nobuteru lived in different worlds, so there was little chance that the two of them would ever meet, and it was even less likely that Takeshi would seek revenge against his old friends. But this did little to comfort Nobuteru. His uneasiness went deeper; it was connected to the fact that he was alive at all.

Some time between Nobuteru's fifty-seventh birthday and the time he nearly choked to death at age seventy, Takeshi found himself sitting in a gloomy bar that seemed to be steeped in dust. He was dead. Unbeknown to Nobuteru, he had been killed in an automobile accident at age fifty-seven. He was no longer crippled; when he assumed his immortal form, his broken body and ruptured organs had been restored. The others he met there, unsure even of their own existence, called the place "Hell". But Takeshi wasn't disturbed about being there. He

14

remembered what a familiar-looking man told him when he arrived:

"You know what Hell is? It's just a place without God. The Japanese don't believe in God to begin with, so what's the difference between this world and the world of the living?"

"I suppose you're right," said Takeshi, without giving the matter much thought.

There were several ghostly figures sitting at tables in the bar, but Takeshi had little interest in them. He seemed to know some of them, but others he didn't recognize at all. People would occasionally stop by to talk, and he got the feeling that he had met everyone in the bar at least once in life, but he wasn't sure.

"Did everyone arrive here recently?" he asked a shabby-looking man, who also seemed familiar.

"No," said the man. "I once met a man who had been here three hundred years. He was the chief retainer of a feudal lord in the late Edo period. People like him are so filled with regret that they'll never get out of here."

"What kind of regret?"

"His master died at the age of six. Just before he died, his master said the word *he*. The man thought it was a command to follow the boy into death, and he pleaded with his feudal lord for permission to kill himself. He was refused, but he committed hara-kiri anyway. When he got here and spoke to his young master, he discovered the boy hadn't said *he* at all. He had said *chi* – his favourite maid was named Chié. The old guy still hasn't recovered. He just wanders around saying, 'I had so many things I wanted to do.' People usually stop caring about that kind of thing once they get here, but not him."

Takeshi realized that not everyone in Hell was connected to him after all. He was also surprised to hear that a six-year-old child was there.

"What's your name? Haven't we met somewhere before?" he asked the man, who had been eyeing Takeshi's well-cut business suit.

"Could be. I was a businessman myself. Before I became homeless, that is. My name's Sasaki."

Sasaki, it turned out, had worked for a client of Shinwa Industries – Takeshi's company. Takeshi was taken aback by this coincidence, but decided not to mention that he had been on the board of directors, since he might have been indirectly responsible for the man losing his job. In fact, Sasaki had met Takeshi once in life, but Sasaki didn't recognize Takeshi without his crutches.

When Yoshitomo Izumi entered the bar, he was startled to see his old boss sitting alone in the middle of the room. While the other figures in the room were nothing but indistinct silhouettes, the figure of Takeshi Uchida was clear as day. What was he doing here? Takeshi had been a good boss, promoting Izumi often and always treating him well. Why was he in Hell?

Izumi walked up to Takeshi. "Hello, sir," he said. "It's me, Izumi."

Takeshi had a talent for laughing loudly and genuinely, even at things that weren't funny. And now, reunited with his subordinate, he laughed the same way he always had when he entertained clients. The situation wasn't without an element of humour; the look on Izumi's face, a mixture of trust and diffidence, was exactly the same as it had been at the office.

17

"A plane crash, was it? Well, have a seat."

In Hell it was possible to view moments in another person's life simply by staring at them. There were no comic-book-style balloons above their head to indicate what they were thinking, nor was it a form of mental telepathy. Instead, the truth was revealed through a kind of vision that crept up from the back of one's mind. So as he sat down, Izumi was astonished to see that Takeshi had had an affair with his wife. He saw everything that had taken place, through Takeshi's eyes, through the eyes of his wife Sachiko and through his own eyes as well.

Takeshi could tell from the expression on Izumi's face that he now knew everything, but Takeshi didn't go on the defensive. He merely nodded calmly.

"So you know," he said.

"Sir…"

Seeing Takeshi without his crutches, Izumi understood that he was looking at Takeshi's immortal form. And although Izumi's own body had been horribly mangled and charred in a plane crash, the fact that he now sat there intact and apparently immortal made it painfully obvious where they both were. Perhaps that was why he felt no anger or hatred towards his boss, and why no feelings of jealousy welled up in his heart. When he thought about it, he hadn't really loved Sachiko anyway. And hadn't he himself betrayed her? But beyond that, Izumi now also realized that his unusually rapid advancement at the company – where he became head of general affairs at the age of forty – had been due largely to Takeshi's support. Sachiko had only agreed to Takeshi's overtures on the condition that he help her husband's career.

In his vision, Izumi had seen Takeshi and his beautiful wife meet at an office party. He saw Sachiko's compassion for the disabled man and her attraction to his refined bearing. He saw the two of them walking in a hotel garden on a Friday evening. And he saw Sachiko and Takeshi as they made love. Everything was revealed to him in minute detail, down to the smell that filled the hotel room. It was the stifling body-heat smell created when a man and a woman come together, bare skin against bare skin. It is a smell no movie or tawdry romance novel can duplicate. And somehow it seems even more pungent when you aren't a part of it.

Although he appreciated Sachiko's beauty in a detached way, Izumi no longer felt any physical attraction to her. This was something that happened to husbands and wives after a while, he thought, and he saw nothing wrong with his obsession with someone else. The other woman was the actress Yumiko Hanawa. Every Wednesday night, Izumi had gone to the Night Walker, a club that Yumiko frequented after hosting her Wednesday-night television variety show. Sometimes she would come close to Izumi's table as she moved like a breeze over the dance floor. Sometimes she and her friends would take seats close to his. And sometimes he would catch a whiff of her perfume or intercept one of her seductive glances. The chance for such a thrill once a week had been enough to fulfil him.

Takeshi found it odd that Izumi's attitude towards him remained unchanged, despite the fact that he had seen the truth of his affair. But maybe that was all part of being in Hell. There didn't seem to be any point in getting angry. Why get jealous? True, Takeshi had been unemotional in life, but had Izumi also been this detached? Takeshi felt a strange closeness to the stolid Izumi next to him.

Then, suddenly, Takeshi was Izumi. He had come home early one afternoon to find a pair of men's shoes in the foyer. His wife's moans greeted him as he crept up the stairs. From the half-open bedroom door came a suffocatingly warm, musky smell and the sound of the bed creaking. He peered into the room to see his own naked buttocks between Sachiko's spread legs. Had this really happened? Had Izumi seen this and somehow repressed it? Or was this Takeshi's own experience, seen through Izumi's eyes? Only in Hell could one experience an erotic vision like this.

Daté ran and ran. He was beginning to think that it would be easier if he were caught and killed. The Ikaruga gang members would surely be waiting for him once he dashed out of the alley and around the corner.

All right, then. Let them come. Get it over with. Wait, no! You only die once. Make the most of it! Some people die without even realizing it, like some poor fool getting his skull crushed by an object dropped from the roof of a building. But not him. He was going to cling to life with everything he had. He was going to savour his death.

Daté turned the corner, and the moment he did so, he was a changed man. It was as if a switch had been flipped in the centre of his fear-addled brain. He was no longer being pursued. He had become the pursuer. He wasn't the prey. He was the hunter. He began to walk slowly, calmly. Where were those Ikaruga sons of bitches? He was going to kill them. And what about Hattori? Still running, no doubt. Then he was going to kill him too. It didn't matter that Hattori was his subordinate. If he put up a fight, he'd beat him to within an inch of his life and then leave him there to die.

He felt like a tiger on the prowl. When he passed people on the street, he stared them in the face, his eyes wild. As he walked, he thought of his family home in the mountains beyond the last stop on the

Yakihata Line. His shoulders were thrown back, and his nostrils were flaring. For the first time in his life, he was a real yakuza.

Hattori, on the other hand, had already been caught. Just after he started running, he collided with a passer-by and fell, hitting his head on the pavement. He was lying on the ground, dazed, when the three Ikaruga gang members got to him. They dragged him into a small bar in the basement of a nearby building.

"We need to use your place for a while," Asahina, the oldest of the three gangsters, said to the *mama-san*. It was obvious that they were well acquainted.

"Just finish before the customers show up," said the *mama-san*, a burly woman of around forty. She didn't seem particularly put out. Perhaps she was used to this.

It was eight o'clock, still early for this area. There was plenty of time before the first customers were expected. Asahina had ordered one of his men to attend to Yuzo's body, and now he had the other two tie Hattori to a chair.

To Hattori, Asahina seemed more fearless than Yuzo ever had. Why couldn't he have served under Asahina instead? If he had joined the Ikaruga gang instead of the Sakaki gang, he could have been one of Asahina's men. Unlike Daté, Hattori hadn't been wild as a boy, and he didn't even like violence. He was just lazy and not very bright and ended up in the Sakaki gang because it seemed like the easiest thing to do.

"Talk. Which gang are you from? Talk, or I'll pour this cleanser down your throat." Asahina knew that threatening to slice up a yakuza's face would have little effect – if anything, scars are a badge of honour – so he grabbed the closest thing at hand to terrorize Hattori. But he needn't have bothered. Hattori immediately told them everything.

The dead man was Yuzo Motoyama, a lieutenant in the Sakaki gang and Hattori's senior, his *aniki-bun*. The man who ran away was Daté, Hattori's immediate superior. Hattori himself was nothing but a thug, the lowest rank in the organization with nobody under him. He would tell them any-thing they wanted to know – just, he pleaded, don't kill him.

But Asahina hadn't brought this pathetic man here just to pry information out of him. He had other interests: he was a sadist, and under his tutelage his men had developed a taste for torture as well. The expression on Hattori's pale, pudgy face made it seem like he was on the verge of tears, and this only inflamed Asahina's desire to inflict pain. But Hattori had spilt his guts so easily that Asahina had no reason to torture him. In the end, his inability to come up with a reason was reason enough.

"Do you really think we brought you here just for that? We're here to have some fun," he taunted.

Asahina twisted his face into a smile, and his two underlings grinned in kind. He ordered them to strip Hattori to the waist, and then, with a carving knife, he made a shallow vertical slash on Hattori's fat belly. Hattori began to sob.

"Does that hurt?" asked Asahina. Hattori's tears excited him, but he quickly realized that robbing Hattori of all hope would take the thrill out of the exercise. "If you cry the right way, I might let you live," he added.

"Cry like a baby," said Yagyu, one of the under-lings. There was no emotion in his voice as he stared vacantly at Hattori. His penis was erect.

"Most Japanese have no religious faith, and they have no one, including their parents, who can serve in God's stead. So if they get even a little power, they start to think of themselves as gods. You might say that Hell exists solely for the purpose of ridding ourselves of that illusion. After all, there's no place that can do that in the world of the living."

This was what Takeshi's acquaintance in Hell had told him, the man who said that Hell was not so different from the world of the living. But had Takeshi known this person in life? Could it be that he only seemed like an acquaintance and that Takeshi had never really known him at all? In Hell it was sometimes difficult to distinguish between memory and imagination, and yet Takeshi had a feeling that there was always a reason when that happened. Maybe the man was a demon or devil trying to teach him the true nature of Hell. Takeshi might have been given a false memory to fool himself into thinking that he knew the man. For all he knew, the man might have been Enma, the lord of the Japanese underworld.

Takeshi was at the beach. Hadn't he been at this beach when he first met the man? It was night, and the beach was lit with floodlights. People in swimsuits were reclining on the sand. The sky was devoid of stars and moon, and the sea was the colour of lead. Hardly anyone was swimming. Takeshi in his business suit was the only one fully dressed. He walked along the beach in a pair of light shoes, freed now from his crutches.

As he walked among the men and women on the beach, he found himself looking for Yuzo. He had never met Yuzo as an adult, but he didn't think it mattered. In Hell it seemed entirely possible to see someone as they had appeared in the distant past. And even if Yuzo were to appear at the age of his death, Takeshi was sure that he would recognize him without difficulty. He had heard from a classmate that Yuzo had been killed after becoming a Yakuza, so he would almost certainly be in Hell, but Takeshi had yet to meet him.

As for Nobuteru, his other childhood friend, Takeshi didn't know if he was alive or dead. He often wondered what kind of conversation the three of them might have if they were reunited. What would he say to the people responsible for crippling him for life? He wasn't sure if he could say everything as he envisioned it, but finding that out would be part of the fun.

Even after meeting Sasaki in that dusty bar, Takeshi had no recollection of meeting him in life. In fact, it was a mistake that Sasaki made in a deal with Takeshi's firm that cost him his job at a construction company and started his long homeless existence. Sasaki's wife Jitsuko had been with him on the streets, and yet for some reason he hadn't seen her in Hell. Why wasn't she here? Surely she had frozen to death with him. Could she not have died after all? Or had she died and gone somewhere else – to heaven or paradise or whatever it was called? She had been a good wife, staying with him no matter what. Maybe she hadn't deserved to go to Hell.

It was bitterly cold the winter that Sasaki died. He and Jitsuko shivered in a tent they had rigged up out of plastic sheeting in a corner of the park. They each had a thin blanket around them, like an oak leaf wrapped around a *mochi*. There was no heat and nothing they could burn; the blankets were all they had. The cold crept up their backs and spread through their bodies to their throbbing heads. The *chitter-chitter-chittering* of their teeth filled the tent. Every sleepless night they were convinced that they would freeze to death, but every morning the sun shone through the tent's thin plastic walls, warming them a little and allowing them finally to drift off to sleep. It was the same day after day.

"It can't be helped. It wasn't your fault," said Sasaki's wife. Her attempts to comfort him were the only bright spot in his life, but they left him feeling worse as he desperately apologized for what happened.

"If only that Izumi hadn't asked for a kickback. He and that cripple supervisor of his – Uchida, I think his name was. They were in cahoots, I bet. I only met Uchida once. I said hello to him in the hallway, and he said, 'I have complete confidence in Izumi.' I know what he meant by that now! He was in on it. I talked it over with Shinoda – he was my supervisor – and we decided not to pay up. But no kickback meant no contract. And I was out of a job, just like that. Shinoda didn't say a word in my defence, the bastard."

"I told you to stop thinking about it. Hate doesn't solve anything."

"But look what I've done to you, leaving you without a home. You didn't have to come here with me."

"Who else would have an ugly woman like me? Where can an old woman like me go?"

And yet Jitsuko had been quite pretty in her youth. A difficult life had aged her beyond her years, making her seem shabby and ugly. Their homelessness was his fault, and yet she was always kind to him. She loved him, and maybe that was the hardest part of all. Her ugliness made her even sadder and more pitiful, magnifying his own love for her. Such a good woman should never have been put in this situation. Not after everything he had already put her through.

"It's cold."

"Yes."

"I feel terrible. My body's like ice. Do you think this is what it's like in the 'eight freezing hells'? We're going to die tonight. I just know it."

"Don't be silly. Soon the sun will come out and warm us up, just like it always does. This spot gets the most sun in the entire park."

Sasaki and his wife never saw another dawn.

Nobuteru's father was a bureaucrat and a strict disciplinarian, but he had never scolded Nobuteru about Takeshi's broken leg. He hadn't even mentioned it. He thought that it was the nature of boys to be rough and rowdy. He was proud of his family line, undistinguished though it may have been, and he couldn't have cared less what happened to the child of some nobody.

Nobuteru joined the track-and-field team when he entered high school after the war. At a party for the new team members, the seniors pressed him to drink. Nobuteru got terribly drunk and awoke the next day with a bad hangover. Somehow he made it through the day. He was to go to dinner with his parents and sister that evening, but feeling ill, he asked to be excused. His father would hear nothing of it. He shouldn't let something like a hangover get the best of him, he said. Did he want to be laughed at when he became a salaryman? Nobuteru was coming to dinner, no matter how sick he felt.

His family sat down at the French restaurant and began to order. Nobuteru's nausea grew worse as his father lectured him. These full-course meals were expensive, he said. Just think of all the children in the world who would never see a meal like this. Nobuteru had better eat, and clean his plate besides.

"But dear, Nobuteru says he's not feeling well," said his mother.

This, coupled with the concerned look on his sister's face, served only to worsen his father's mood. "He's going to eat if we have to stay here all night. When he gets a job, he'll have to deal with situations like this all the time. He needs to learn this lesson now. No son of mine is going to be mollycoddled."

The table was silent as the food was served. Nobuteru jumped up from the table to go to the toilet.

"Sit down! We're still eating!" shouted his father, paying no attention to the stares he was attracting. "Where are your manners?"

Lips squeezed tightly together, Nobuteru sat back down. Finally he could hold back no longer, and in one explosive burst he vomited everything in his belly onto the table and floor. His father was livid. He bellowed, stood up from the table, and stomped out of the restaurant. He made no apology to the staff for his son's mess.

That was fifty-five years ago, but Nobuteru remembered the night as clearly as anything. Had this experience caused his father to rethink his stubbornness? Nobuteru didn't think so. It might actually have made it worse. But rather than learning from his father's behaviour, Nobuteru realized that he had grown up to be no different.

He tried to maintain at least the appearance of reasonableness, but his dislike for young people – a common trait among old men – grew more intense with each passing year. Just the way young people talked irritated him. And watching them sing their songs on television was enough to put him in a foul mood – mostly because he could make neither head nor tail of the lyrics.

He would go to bookstores in search of something well-written and elegant, but manga was all he could find. The only things resembling books had garish covers and sat on shelves once reserved for literature. They had titles like *Broadband KAP-4 Basics*, *New Developments in Galaxy Net*, *Master Secretarial Software* and *All about 'Seducing Sophia': The Ultimate Guide to Your Virtual Girlfriend*.

It gave him a headache. Was there nothing for him to read? He would consider asking the store staff for help, but everyone was young and he couldn't bear the look they always gave him – the look that said, "What are you talking about?" So he would walk out of the store without a word. No doubt that was what they wanted anyway.

"Which will you take, the high road or the low road?"

"Which one is longer?"

"They're both short."

Was this a memory from one of Nobuteru's previous lives? Or a conversation he had with an unseen being before he was born? And how had he chosen? He thought that it was probably the low road. It did seem more interesting. But if that were the case, then how had he managed to live so long? Still, it was true that he hadn't always taken the low road. He had sometimes walked on the proverbial "sunny side of the street". He had been president of several companies, if only in name, and despite the low salary, he had even got a legitimate job in an effort to turn over a new leaf when his son was born.

But the temptations of the low road were great. His dealings with the underworld had given him an income far greater than any salaryman's. His son was now over thirty and rarely came home except to ask for money. It was just as well that he hadn't knocked himself out working a straight job for a son like that.

He got a licence to teach Japanese, but taught for less than a year before giving up the profession. He floated in and out of various enterprises; real-estate scams, business rackets, pyramid schemes, underground pornography rings – he did it all. He finally managed to build up a small nest egg managing a hostess club with a dozen or so girls, some under-age, some foreign. He closed the club down when he got wind of a raid.

Yuzo had always taken the low road and had died young. Takeshi had always taken the high road, but had he lived any longer? He couldn't be dead too, could he? The thought that he might be the only one of them left alive was too lonely for Nobuteru to contemplate.

Had the familiar-looking man been right? Was Hell really just a place without God? Why did everything for which Takeshi had worked so hard now seem silly? Why did everything he suffered for and agonized over in his youth now seem laughable? Everyone who came to Hell seemed to feel the same way, and not just about their own lives. Everything that had happened in the real world – everything that must still be happening there – seemed utterly insignificant. Could that be the true nature of Hell? To make people forget their attachments to their previous lives? Was that the real reason for Hell's existence?

Takeshi was sitting at an expensive restaurant with a high ceiling. It wasn't particularly large; there were no more than ten tables altogether. He ordered a few of his favourite dishes, but found the food vaguely unsatisfying: he hadn't been very hungry and everything always tasted the same – exactly as he remembered it in life. He was alone, but everyone else sat in groups of two or three. They must have been friends who had often gone to this kind of restaurant together in life. Takeshi had no such friends. He always went to restaurants alone so that he could devote his full attention to the food.

He hadn't seen Sasaki since their first meeting, and in any case Sasaki would hardly fit in at a restaurant like this. He was probably wandering around looking for that wife of his who froze to death with him. He hadn't seen Izumi either. Izumi at least wouldn't have been out of place there, but Takeshi was trying his best not to think about him. When you thought about people in Hell, they had a nasty habit of appearing, and Takeshi didn't think he could bear sharing a meal with Izumi. Izumi probably felt the same way.

Two well-dressed men about Takeshi's age were sitting down at the next table. One had a Ronald Coleman moustache, and seemed to have brought with him a boy in tattered clothes and dirty canvas shoes. The boy sat down awkwardly between the two men, who faced each other across the table. Takeshi stiffened. The boy looked just like Yuzo!

"I brought this war orphan from the past," the first man said to the second man, who was wearing black-rimmed glasses. "He was in the same situation that I was in as a boy. I'm not sure it was good idea, bringing him here, but I couldn't help myself."

It really was Yuzo! Or to be exact, Yuzo from the period about a year after Takeshi had last seen him. His family must have been killed in the air raids. Small wonder he became a yakuza. Takeshi couldn't take his eyes off him. The boy's hungry eyes darted around the room, seeing Takeshi but not recognizing him.

"So it's almost like going back to buy a decent meal for yourself when you were starving as a boy," said the second man.

"I suppose you could say that." The two men exchanged smiles.

Could this man really have brought Yuzo to Hell from the real world? At first, Takeshi thought that his childhood memories had given Yuzo his youthful appearance. But no, it was clear he wasn't an adult who had died and come to Hell. He had to be Yuzo as a boy, somehow plucked from the real world's past. Were such things possible in Hell?

Takeshi was perplexed. If Hell was a place without God, then who was in charge of it? The Devil? He refused to believe that. Both God and the Devil were creations of the human mind. But couldn't that also be true of Hell itself? Couldn't Hell just exist in Takeshi's mind? If that were the case, the possibilities were endless: Takeshi's organs might have been crushed in the accident, but his brain preserved. His broken body could be in some kind of sterile life-support capsule. He could be dreaming all of this. Or he could even be in an artificial world – a computer-generated meta-reality that someone had created.

The waiter arrived and took the orders of the two

men. He did it very naturally; he had probably been a waiter in life as well. Takeshi wondered if there was anywhere in Hell that would suit him as well as this restaurant seemed to suit the waiter. Perhaps Takeshi was best suited to wandering from place to place, as he had been doing since coming here.

Yuzo squirmed in his chair as the men spoke to the waiter. He seemed to have no idea what they were ordering, but when he heard words like "chicken" and "duck" mentioned, he would look imploringly at the men, as if saying, "Please order one of those for me!" When the men were done ordering and the waiter was about to leave, Yuzo, his eyes open wide, shouted in a panic:

"Meat! Meat! Meat! Meat!"

"Don't shout," said the first man, making a face.

"I will be bringing meat, sir," said the waiter expressionlessly before retreating towards the kitchen.

"A 'sirloin' is a cut of beef," said the second man to Yuzo. He turned to the first man and went on, "Come to think of it, all we said was 'beef' back then. We never used words like 'sirloin' or 'roast', did we?"

"All we had was ground beef that could've come from any part of the cow. And we were lucky to get even that."

Takeshi himself had never eaten meat as a child. His family had been well off by the standards of the time, but even they had been close to starvation. People thought it lavish to have an actual bowl of rice instead of a watery broth with a few grains of rice at the bottom of the bowl. If you poured soy sauce over a bowl of hot rice and stirred it around, you could almost believe you were having the impossible treat of rice mixed with a raw egg. As a war orphan, Yuzo would have been lucky to eat a crust of bread a day.

The waiter brought out the appetizer. It was fish carpaccio. Yuzo put his mouth to the edge of the plate and began to shovel the fish into his mouth.

"What are you doing?" said the first man. "Eat your food this way."

Yuzo paid no attention. He picked up the plate and stuffed the rest of the fish into his mouth, then he licked the dressing from the plate.

"What atrocious manners," said the second man with a smile. "If you like the dressing so much,

41

break off a piece of bread and – say, that's odd. What happened to the bread?"

All of the bread in the basket had disappeared. Yuzo had stuffed it into his pockets.

"You mustn't do that," said the first man, beginning to look annoyed. "Put the bread back in the basket."

Yuzo ignored him. He grabbed the uneaten watercress and radish sprouts off the men's plates and stuffed them into his mouth. Then he picked up their plates and licked them clean.

"If you're going to behave like that, I won't be taking you out to dinner again," said the first man sternly. "So what will it be? Is it all right if you never get to come here again? Or do you want to learn some manners?"

Yuzo wept as he silently removed a piece of bread from his pocket and began to wolf it down. The expression on his face seemed to say, "I can't help myself. Can't you see I'm starving?"

The waiter appeared. "Shall I bring another basket of bread, sir?"

"Ah, yes please. Wait, on second thought, he'll just

take it all again. Just put some on our plates when you bring our main courses."

"Very good, sir."

"He'll still take it, you know," said the second man.

"The little brat," spat the first man. "When I was his age, I was starving too, but I'd like to think I still had manners and exercised self-control."

There was no change in young Yuzo's behaviour after the soup arrived. With his eyes wide open, he picked up his bowl with both hands, brought it to his mouth, and drank the soup down in a few short gulps, paying no attention to how hot it was. When he was done, he licked the bowl. He reached out for the men's bowls, but the second man smacked the back of his hand with the flat of his knife. Yuzo glared at him as if he wanted to bite him.

Yes, this was Hell. That Yuzo would join a gang after being subjected to such cruelty seemed hardly surprising. He would almost certainly never be brought to a restaurant like this again. He probably knew that too, which was why he saw no point in trying to improve his manners. What would happen when the waiter brought their steaks? In his current state, Yuzo might try to eat the leftovers off Takeshi's plate as well. Takeshi didn't think he could bear to watch that. He summoned the waiter for his bill. There was always the same amount of money in his wallet, even after he spent some.

But these worldly gentlemen here with Yuzo – what was their story? Why were they in Hell? As Takeshi left the restaurant, he peeked into their minds. They were members of the board of directors of a bank, and had got rich by padding their pensions just before retiring.

Takeshi suddenly found himself longing to see Izumi again. With Izumi, he might at least be able to have a moderately intelligent conversation and forget his current mood. But where could Izumi be? Takeshi started walking in the direction of some high-rise buildings that resembled offices. Yes, they were office buildings. Perhaps Izumi was there.

But at that moment Izumi was riding the train. He was one of a number of passengers sitting on a train very similar to the ones that he had once ridden to work. As he was boarding the train, he noticed Sasaki getting into the same car, so he quickly retreated to the adjacent car. He saw in Sasaki's mind that his demand for a kickback had got Sasaki fired, and he saw how Sasaki died. It was a grim way to go, but Izumi felt no guilt or sympathy for the man. If he met Sasaki face to face, he would have to say how terrible he felt and how sorry he was, but of course that wasn't true at all. He had lost all such feelings since coming to Hell. And Sasaki was unlikely to confront Izumi anyway. They were in Hell. What good would it do to bring up resentments from life?

Sasaki seemed terribly run-down, but then Izumi realized that Sasaki was wearing the same drab business suit he had always worn. The only difference was that he wasn't wearing a tie. Izumi could have said something to Sasaki, but the truth was he didn't care one way or the other about him. Izumi had other things on his mind; he was lost in memories and he wanted to stay lost. That was the real reason he had stayed away from Sasaki. In his mind, Izumi was back at the Night Walker.

* * *

Yumiko Hanawa, the host of the television variety show *Premiere 21*, was arriving at the Night Walker as she did every Wednesday night after filming was over. She was accompanied by her producer Nishizawa, the guests of the show that night and various others – about ten people in all. She led the way across the club's dance floor, drawing stares from customers sitting at the tables. Trailing her was her entourage, some wearing flashy stage costumes, others in trendy casual wear, and others, like her manager and the TV-station staff, in business suits. Izumi had been at the club, waiting. He had got a table next to a section of booths that had remained empty all night, hoping that they were reserved for Yumiko and her group. He wasn't disappointed.

"You see that businessman sitting next to us?" Konzo Ichikawa, a young kabuki actor, whispered to Yumiko once they were seated. Konzo didn't have a distinguished kabuki family pedigree, but he was a rising star of the theatre and his sense of humour had landed him guest spots on *Premiere 21* several times. "I've seen him here a lot. He's always alone."

"Him? Oh, he's one of my fans. The manager says he's here every Wednesday."

"I knew it." A mischievous gleam entered Konzo's eyes. "He can't take his eyes off you."

"Why don't you take pity on the poor guy?" chuckled Mamoru Kashiwazaki, one of the show's regular guests. He was a singer and a well-known practical joker. "Sleep with him, and he'll lose his mind trying to satisfy your every whim. I know the type."

"That would be a hoot," said Osanai, Kashiwazaki's manager. He quite liked the idea. "Why don't you talk to him? I want to see him squirm."

"Men!" Yumiko replied, looking up at the ceiling with false exasperation. There was a sparkle in her eyes; she was not uninterested.

"I'd like to see how he acts myself!" Kashiwazaki said, tapping Mayumi Shibata, the assistant host, on her back. "Come on. You want to see it too, don't you?"

"Oh, sure," said Shibata unenthusiastically. "Definitely."

47

"I'd sleep with him if I was a woman," said Konzo. "I'd love to watch him fall to pieces. I could use it as inspiration for my art."

In the next booth, the novelist Yoshio Torikai was grumbling to Nishizawa, the producer of the show, about a certain critic. Nishizawa had no connection to the literary world and was the only one whom Torikai could complain to. "He trashed every one of my books. So when I met him at a party, I confronted him about it. And you know what he said? He said, 'Why don't you write a rebuttal? That way you'll get paid something and I'll get paid to respond. So we both win, right?' That's all it was. These guys are hacks. They write this rubbish for the money."

"Mind if I join you?"

Izumi looked up to find Yumiko standing in front of his table in her beige dress. The blood in his body started to fizz like soda pop. He had noticed Yumiko and her friends peering at him from the next table, whispering among themselves, but he never dreamt that Yumiko would actually come over and talk to him. He was speechless. He wanted to say "of course" as he made a place for her to sit, but the words stuck in his throat and he succeeded only in knocking over his whisky-and-water. He smiled and nodded eagerly as he wiped the table with his handkerchief. Yumiko sat down beside him, paying no attention to the damp patch on the sofa. The breeze caused by her movement touched Izumi's face. It smelt of the perfume Poison. He felt the sofa give slightly under the weight of her body.

"You come here often, don't you?"

"Yes, every Wednesday."

"You wouldn't be coming to see me, would you?"

"You might say that. Uh... ha ha ha." Izumi motioned for the waiter and knocked over his glass again.

Izumi could see the group at the next table looking down at their hands, their shoulders shaking with laughter. But he couldn't worry about them – the waiter had just arrived and he wanted to order a drink for Yumiko. To do that, he would have to ask her what she wanted. And then he would tell her how he had longed for her. And then he would tell her how this was like a dream come true. And then he would somehow have to survive the pain in his chest. And... And... And...

After a bit, the conversation between Izumi and Yumiko relaxed, and her friends lost interest in them. Izumi had said how he had first seen Yumiko when she had played the lead in the travelling production of *The Diary of Anne Frank* and that he had been a devoted fan of hers ever since. Yumiko was telling him what a hellish experience it was.

"I've got a long nose like a Jew, don't you think? I suppose that's why they picked me for the part, but I wish I never auditioned for it. I really do. We played our first month in Tokyo and it was a big success. And sure, I was happy about that. But then we went on tour. We played prefectural halls, cultural centres, community centres, even school auditoriums. I think we must have played every prefecture in the country. Everyone wanted to see a play based on such a famous story. And of course junior-high and high-school groups came, too, so it was a full house everywhere we went. I don't remember how many places we played, but we were on the road for three years. Three years! You can't imagine how terrible it was! Day after day, the same lines, the same stage directions. Oh, they'd have to make a few changes depending on the size and shape of the stage, but that was it. I thought I'd go out of my mind with boredom!"

Yumiko could not stop talking about how the experience had scarred her so deeply. Even in her hotel room later, as she was taking off her clothes, she kept telling Izumi about it. "Perform, travel, perform, travel, perform, travel, rest, perform, perform, travel, rest. That's what our schedule was like. And of course, we were out in the middle of nowhere, so there was nothing we could do even on our days off. Come on, get your clothes off. Quite a few cast members quit, but I was the lead. They couldn't find a replacement for me so easily, and there were people coming just to see me play Anne, or at least that's what they told me. I did that for three years! Can you imagine? I enjoyed the audience's applause for the first three months or so, but that was it. After that, no excitement, nothing. I was just going through the motions like a machine, day after day. Hurry up, get your clothes off, we don't have all night."

Izumi was sitting on the bed, entranced. Yumiko

had said she was bored always being with the same crowd, so why didn't they go back to her hotel? She said goodbye to group, and they had left, just like that. Her friends stared blankly at her as she walked out of the club; they hadn't expected her to go through with it. And now she stood nude in front of the adoring Izumi. She walked around the room, still talking, and then stopped when she caught a glimpse of herself in the full-length mirror.

"Ah, eternal beauty," she smiled.

Yumiko struck a few poses before the mirror, started to talk again, then walked over to Izumi and lay down on the bed. She prompted him to take off his clothes again, and Izumi at last began to undress. His heart was racing. He had no idea what Yumiko was saying any more. His eyes were consuming her body. She had lain down on top of the sheets, giving Izumi a full view of the black of her pubic hair and the pink of her genitals. He kneeled on the bed and began to inch his way up her body. They began to make love. But Yumiko would not stop talking.

"I can't bear to think about it any more. Always the same faces. Always the same sets. Even the audiences were always the same. It was a nightmare. Please, Mister… Izumi – that is your name, yes? – make me forget! Make me forget everything!"

Despite the dreariness of the moment, Izumi ejaculated within five seconds.

"Well, well, well. Did we have a little problem there?" said the chubby woman sitting across from Izumi on the train. She looked about sixty years old. He didn't know how long she had been there.

"Mind your own business," Izumi said angrily. He glared at her. But he wasn't particularly angry or embarrassed. He was just surprised how, even in Hell, this woman could spy on a total stranger's private reminiscences.

The woman actually seemed quite amiable. She tried to placate him, the smile never leaving her face. "I'm sorry. I used to be a psychic, you see. And ever since I came here, my powers have got much stronger. Sometimes I get a bit carried away."

"You were a psychic?" said Izumi, his interest piqued as he looked into her own past. "And you were murdered? Who killed you?"

"A murderer."

"Well, that goes without saying. If he killed you, then he's a murderer, isn't he?"

"No, that's not what I mean." The old woman's slightly flaccid jowls jiggled as she shook her head. She seemed annoyed by Izumi's inferior powers of intuition.

"Let me start at the beginning," she said. "I was living in Sendai, where I was famous for finding lost objects, and one day the police came to me for help. They were sure that a missing woman had been murdered, but they had no body and no leads and didn't know what to do. So they asked me to help them, and I did. They found her body buried way up in the mountains, just as I told them. The police hunted for her killer, but they didn't have any luck. They must have felt they would lose face if they didn't arrest somebody, so they decided that *I* was the killer! Can you believe that? They said that only the killer could have known where the body was buried. They questioned me for days and days. I just about lost my mind. They told me that if I was innocent, I should use my powers to help them find the real killer. But my speciality is finding lost things. I'm no good at finding murderers. Luckily, they caught the killer just then. A policeman had been going door to door asking about a completely unrelated case, and when he got to the killer's house, the guy panicked and ran.

"That was twenty years ago. By that I mean twenty years before my death. The next part happened just a little while ago – about a week before I died. A detective came to see me, wanting help finding the body of a murder victim – again. The detective was young and didn't know my history with the police. I said that I was fed up with helping the police and told him my story. 'Nothing like that will happen this time,' he said. 'I promise you.'

"The media found out about this, and television cameras showed up, so I figured it would be all right. But there was no way I was going to help the police until they apologized for what happened before. So I turned him down. They showed that part on television, and even had a voice-over talking about my experience with the police. The next night I was killed. The murderer was afraid I was going to expose him. He came to my house and beat me to death. It's a shame that psychics can never tell what's going to happen to themselves, isn't it? But the police were able to get a lead on the murderer because of what happened to me, and they finally caught him. The media had a field day with that, let me tell you." Having finished her story, the woman laughed as if she had been talking about someone else the whole time.

Daté continued walking from one backstreet to another, his face contorted into a demented expression. He no longer tried to avoid the other pedestrians, even if they were walking directly towards him. If they didn't get out of his way, he ploughed right into them. He was stumbling away from one such collision when he happened to hear the song 'Tokyo Dodonpa Girl' playing in a store, and from that point on hummed the song under his breath. His feet also succumbed to the rhythm of the song, tracing out the steps of the *dodonpa* as he walked, his eyes gazing fixedly up at the sky.

Dodonpa! Dodonpa! Dodonpa!
It's lit a fire in my heart
That nothing can put out!

Customers had not yet arrived at the small basement bar where Hattori was being tortured.
Asahina had removed Hattori's trousers and ripped
off his underwear, which was filthy from Hattori's
repeated shitting and pissing his pants. The burly
mama-san grew more and more willing to be of
assistance as the torture went on. When asked for
a carving knife, she was quite happy to hand one
over; when asked for a chopping board, she merrily
fetched that as well. When Asahina ordered her
to make Hattori's shrivelled penis erect, she com-
plied, diligently kneading, squeezing and stroking
his member.

Hattori was a mess. He had been crying from the
cigarette burns all over his naked body and from
the hot needles inserted under his fingernails, and
now, his mind clouded with pain, he began to babble at the top of his lungs, his words approaching a
bestial scream that even he didn't understand.

"It stings it stings the black black pain in my fingers it burns! But I gotta hold on gotta hold on don't put anything in my cigarette holes don't put anything in me! I'm gonna die gonna die gonna die my head's so hot I feel like I'm goin' crazy yes yes yes crazy crazy what am I gonna do what am I gonna do stop please stop. "

The bar was filled with the smell of Hattori's shit and piss and blood and the sweat of the men torturing him. Tired from their exertions, the three gangsters had been resting on the couch, but Asahina roused himself when he saw that Hattori's penis had become fully erect. He slid the cutting board under Hattori's member and pressed it down on the board. He held the carving knife in his other hand and made as if he was about to slice Hattori's penis off at the base. Seeing this, Hattori howled desperately, pissing himself all over again.

"No! Anything but that! I know what you're gonna do I know I know I gotta be strong be strong but I can't take it any more I can't take it can't take it can't take it I'm gonna die! Is this goodbye is it really goodbye please I can't say goodbye to my little friend not him don't don't please no! Tell me how you want me to cry I'll cry I'll cry good any way you want!"

Asahina's underlings felt a stirring in their own crotches as they watched Hattori babble like a baby. They got up slowly from the couch and threw the whisky in their glasses onto Hattori's naked bleeding body. Hattori screamed and writhed some more.

"Hot hot hot hothothot! Blood whirlpools in my cigarette burns! I'm gonna die die die my fingertips are gone gone gone can I go crazy now? Is that all right? My head feels so strange…"

The *mama-san* was entranced. Her eyes began to sparkle, and then she cried out, having come to a decision. She twirled the dangling sleeves of her kimono around her forearms and went behind the counter to write something on a piece of paper. She went up the stairs to the ground floor and pasted the paper on the glass door with a smack. The sign read:

CLOSED – PRIVATE PARTY TONIGHT

* * *

Daté was asleep. Exhausted from all the running and strutting around, he lay in a narrow dead-end alley, arms curled around a large black dog. He would have nowhere to run if the Ikaruga gang found him there. He had fallen to the ground as soon as he ran into the alley and saw that it was a dead end. Some time afterwards, a black creature came up to him and licked his cheek. Daté embraced the creature passionately, as if it were his last chance to touch another living thing, and soon drifted into a sweet deep sleep.

He was dreaming. Dreaming of Yuzo. Yuzo was sitting across from him at their usual coffee shop. No, the coffee shop didn't really exist. It was just their "usual coffee shop" in Daté's dreams.

"Oh, that's right," he thought in the dream. "Yuzo's been killed. Does that mean that I'm dead too? Is that why I'm here with him now? Or are my dreams connected to the afterlife? I was so tired that I just dropped off to sleep, and now I'm having my favourite dream about being here with Yuzo in our usual coffee shop. I love this dream. I might not mind dying if it could be like this. I might even be dead already, but that's okay with me. If I'm alive, all I have to look forward to is people hurting me and then dying anyway. Yeah, I hope I am dead." Yuzo smiled at Daté as if he could hear what he'd been thinking.

"Hey, Weasel. You're not gunnin' for my job, are you?"

"Who, me? I'm just a weasel."

Yuzo laughed and gave Daté an apple. Daté picked up a knife and began to peel the apple clumsily, but the white of the apple's flesh did not appear. Did this apple have especially thick skin? He made a deeper incision into the apple, but it was still red. Finally he understood. Yuzo had given him an apple that was red to the core. He cut it in two. Just as he thought, the apple was a dark red throughout, almost as if it were made of nothing but skin. Daté complained to Yuzo, a note of entreaty in his voice:

"Hey, what's the big idea? Why did you give me an apple like this?"

Yuzo gave him an innocent look and turned away. He was staring out the window with an expression that seemed to say, "Don't bother me with the petty details of the real world."

"He really is dead," thought Daté.

He spoke to Yuzo tearfully. "Yuzo, I bet it hurt. When you were killed, I mean. I bet it hurt. Huh, Yuzo?"

Getting stabbed in the stomach brought back familiar feelings for Yuzo. He had often experienced pain as a boy, but it was always nothing more than a brief acrid taste in his mouth that soon faded. This time the bitterness lingered, spreading throughout his entire mouth. Yuzo finally recognized it as the taste of death. He had been tasting death little by little ever since he was a child. He slumped forwards and fell to his knees at the feet of the man who stabbed him, angrier at this humiliating position than at his killer. He tried to bite the man's ankles, but only managed to open his eyes. His body would not obey.

Suddenly the pain was gone and Yuzo was standing in the street once again. Everyone else had vanished and the gash in his stomach was gone, but the stores lining the street looked just the same. Their lights were on and their signs were lit, and yet it was so quiet that Yuzo thought he had been struck deaf.

There was no hint of the commotion of moments before. He was dead; that much was clear. Otherwise how could all his anger and hate have disappeared? But where was he? Surely he would understand everything once he turned the corner onto the main street. He began to walk in that direction, taking long purposeful strides.

He left the alley and walked for a few moments before finding himself in a building of cold concrete. He was on the second floor of Yomogawa Primary School, which he attended until his parents died. Was he a spirit or a ghost? Was he now haunting the places that were important to him in life?

He walked towards the stairway and was about to descend, when he froze in his tracks. A man about the same age as Yuzo was standing on the landing looking up at him.

"We used to play here all the time, didn't we?" he said, smiling openly.

The man had no crutches. Was it Nobuteru? No, he was sure it was Takeshi. But how did Yuzo know this? Was that the way things worked in this world? And what was this world anyway? Hell? If so, then

Takeshi must have died before him. But didn't he need his crutches?

As Takeshi slowly climbed the stairs towards him, Yuzo realized that Takeshi had in fact died much later than him and only appeared to be Yuzo's age. And he realized that he no longer had any need for crutches there. He didn't understand how he knew this – he just did. His legs were weak as he faced the friend whom he had hurt so badly. He hoped Takeshi had forgotten his grudges from his previous life, just as he had. Standing in his business suit in front of Yuzo, Takeshi appeared businesslike almost to the point of ostentation. A faint, refined-looking smile came over his handsome features.

"I got bullied terribly in junior high, you know."

Could it be that life and death weren't cut off from each other after all, but were in fact connected in the smoothest, most natural way imaginable? Nobuteru had begun to think so. This had probably been true throughout history, but the closer one got to the present day, the easier it seemed to be to cross over this line without even realizing it. It almost seemed possible to travel between the world of the dead and that of the living.

How else could he explain what had been happening to him? Because Nobuteru had been associated with several different industries, he received many party invitations, even in his retirement. He would be talking to an acquaintance in a noisy banquet hall when he'd spot someone he was certain was long dead. Whenever this happened he would stop and stare dumbly at them – or, as a younger man might say, "freeze up".

There were any number of reasons why he had thought the other person was dead, or there could be no reason at all. Sometimes it was due to an off-hand comment he'd heard, like "Who knows? He may have already passed on." Still, sometimes he was positive that he had read the person's obituary.

Nobuteru had often been on the receiving end of this look as well. He would see someone staring at him and think, "Ah, I've been mistaken for someone who's dead." Or maybe the person had thought Nobuteru himself was dead. It didn't matter. Industries once dominated by young people grew old too, and in a rapidly greying society it was hard to keep track of who was living and who was dead.

The world seemed obsessed with health, with living longer. "Smoking can be hazardous to your health," they said, and so people stopped smoking. But what were they to do with their longer lives? Play croquet? Go into nursing homes? Keep on living until they grew feeble and stinking of old age? And then what?

At these parties sometimes Nobuteru would run into a girl from one of the clubs he had frequented. He'd always find himself thinking: "She's got so old." And as she rubbed up against him, squealing with delight at seeing him after such a long time, she was probably thinking, "Oh, he's turned into such an old man."

At one party a man just collapsed and died. A crowd of greying heads peered down at the pale man lying on the floor. It was clear from the looks on their faces that they were all imagining themselves in his position.

Dead people were all that Nobuteru dreamt about. Maybe it was because most of the people he really cared about were dead. Of course in his dreams they usually were still alive, but sometimes they were dead, and sometimes he couldn't tell one way or the other. He was always confused when he awoke from these dreams, unsure if he himself were still alive.

Once Nobuteru fell into the river near his apartment. He had been in a crowd watching a thrashing school of mullet that had appeared out of the blue. A group of primary-school students pushed from the rear, trying to get a better look, knocking Nobuteru into the river six feet below.

He ended up in the middle of the teeming fish. For a moment he was terrified they would eat him, but then he remembered that mullet eat only plankton. And in any case he knew how to swim. But as he tried to get back to the river bank, the fish bumped up against him, keeping him from making any progress.

He was carried ten yards downstream before he grabbed hold of the concrete embankment and climbed out. A disgusting slime covered his body. He laughed to himself at the absurdity of the situation. Everyone on shore was laughing too, and yet the experience was precious to him. Even after returning to his apartment looking like a drowned rat, he felt an odd satisfaction. If he hadn't known how to swim, he might have drowned. In the end, all he lost were his sandals.

Nobuteru had always thought that, of all the ways to die, drowning was among the most unpleasant, but now he wondered if drowning didn't allow people just to go beneath the surface and slip calmly into death. Maybe people who longed for death would experience such relief that their brain emitted a natural anaesthetic, letting death come quickly and painlessly. There were worse ways to go.

Which magazine had he read it in? Sasaki couldn't remember the magazine, much less the title of the short story or the name of the author. Nevertheless, he would find himself remembering the story from time to time. For some reason it stuck with him, and he thought of it again as he sat on the train looking out at the passing suburban scenery. The protagonist was a man who had thrown an appliance into the bathtub and electrocuted his wife. When the man himself died, he went to Hell, and of course it was the proverbial burning inferno. As the man walked the hot and humid streets of Hell, he began to sweat and his throat grew parched. Ahead of him he spotted a bar. He went inside, but it was just as hot and humid in the bar as it had been outdoors. He ordered a beer from the bartender. The beer was warm.

"I'd like a colder beer, if you don't mind," said the man.

"That's the only kind of beer we've got," replied the bartender.

Drinking the beer just made the man's discomfort worse. Sweat began to pour out of his body. Desperate, the man begged the bartender, "Please, don't you have any beer that's cold?"

But the bartender smiled toothily and said, "We only have warm beer."

That was all there was to the story, but it had a profound effect on Sasaki. It could have been the hot summer day when he first read the story, but he recalled how he himself was sweating profusely, unable to stand the heat. As he sat on the train, he couldn't help but think of similarities between his Hell and the one described in the story.

Every seat of the train was taken, and the aisles were full. Sasaki was lucky to have a seat. When the man standing in front of him left to claim an empty seat, he discovered that his wife was sitting directly across the aisle from him. She was dressed in the same plain clothes she had worn in life, and she seemed to be drowsing. Sasaki was taken aback. His wife had done nothing wrong. What was she doing in Hell? But of course the woman whom he had frozen to death with had never been far from his mind. He timidly called out her name:

"Jitsuko."

Sasaki's wife opened her eyes sleepily and looked at him. She smiled faintly as if she had known he was there all along, and then closed her eyes and went back to sleep. It was just as it had always been when they had ridden the train together in life. Sasaki was disappointed that she didn't seem happier to see him, but at the same time he felt relief. At least she was here with him, even if it didn't change anything. And he supposed her reaction was understandable – no one, including Sasaki himself, felt the kind of strong emotions that they might have felt in the real world.

He sat absorbed in thought, staring at his wife's sleeping face until the train pulled into the station. Jitsuko raised her head drowsily, looked out the window, then slowly stood up and walked towards the door without a glance in Sasaki's direction. Had she forgotten that he was sitting across from her? Sasaki got up to follow her, but the passengers boarding the train came between them and he momentarily lost sight of her. Then the doors shut, leaving him still inside the train. Had she got off? He couldn't see her on the platform.

Standing near the doors of the train was a high-school girl in a navy-blue uniform with a short, tartan-checked skirt. She was looking out the window. Sasaki couldn't see her face, but her standing there stirred a memory in him. He remembered how he used to stand close to girls like this on the train, rub against them and fondle them, snaking his hand up their skirts. He had molested countless girls just like this girl on trains just like this train. He had done it again and again and again, completely unable to control himself. Thinking back, he was surprised that he was never arrested. He thought of the pain he had caused those girls, and he was suddenly filled with regret. Maybe the girl in front of him was actually his wife. Maybe she was there to remind him of what he had done. It didn't matter. What was important was that he was sorry for what he had done. He began to walk slowly down the centre of the train, looking for an empty seat. It was lucky he hadn't gone any further. He had certainly daydreamed about doing worse things.

Past crimes. Cravings long forgotten. Repressed appetites that had never found their way to the surface. Dark desires he had been unaware of. Sasaki began to think that Hell existed to remind him of these malevolent tendencies. If that were the case, then Hell was a world that surpassed the conscious mind, a world where elements of the psyche took on physical form. But apart from that, it really seemed no different from life.

There weren't many young people in Hell, but occasionally Takeshi would encounter young boys. Most seemed innocent and incapable of any real sin, and when he talked to them, he would find that they were guilty of nothing more than a childish prank. How were people chosen to go to Hell? The three intelligent-looking boys he saw skipping stones on the river bank hardly seemed the type to have committed a serious crime. He climbed down to the river bank and called out to them.

"You're so young. How did you die? I haven't seen many boys your age around here."

The boys calmly turned towards him and smiled good-naturedly. They began to speak in turn.

"We're playing in the mountains—"

"On a *torokko* we found on the train tracks."

"A *torroko*?" asked Takeshi. "You mean one of those handcars that you move by pumping the handle up and down?"

The boys ignored him and continued talking.

"Come on. Maybe we can get it moving."

"We all get on."

"We take off the brakes and get it moving on the rails."

"*Torokko torokko* it's slow at first."

"*Torokko torokko* there are rocky hills all around us *torokko torokko* the tracks go up and down *torokko*

torokko now it's going downhill a bit *torokko torokko* make it go faster faster."

"*Torokko torokko* this hill's pretty steep *torokko torokko* it's going fast fast *torokko torokko* there's a cliff to the right *torokko torokko* I can see the valley floor *torokko torokko* I'm scared I'm scared *torokko torokko* it's so fast so fast *torokko torokko* I can see a forest up ahead."

"It's such a big forest *torokko torokko* the wind's rushing past us *torokko torokko* we're really moving now *torokko torokko* how far will we go? *torokko torokko* we've come off the rails *torokko torokko* we're going into the forest *torokko torokko* there are trees all around us *torokko torokko* how can we stop this thing? *torokko torokko* we're going so fast *torokko torokko* I can't breathe *torokko torokko* it won't stop *torokko torokko* I feel dizzy *torokko torokko*."

"*Torokko torokko* somebody save us *torokko torokko* somebody stop this thing *torokko torokko* I can't look *torokko torokko* we hit a tree *torokko torokko* but we're still going *torokko torokko* we just tore through some grass *torokko torokko* it's like a storm of grass around us *torokko torokko* there's a cliff up ahead *torokko torokko* oh no oh no *torokko torokko* we're gonna fall *torokko torokko* we're gonna die *torokko torokko* we fall off the cliff *torokko torokko* the valley floor is below us *torokko torokko* we're upside down *torokko torokko* we're falling into a river *torokko torokko* we're in the river *torokko torokko* but it still won't stop *torokko torokko* what happened? *torokko torokko* we're dead *torokko torokko* and now we're in Hell."

Izumi was lying on the bed in his hotel room, thinking about his wife Sachiko. She had never really loved him. She hadn't slept with his boss to help his career; she'd done it to satisfy her own vanity. She could have gone with him to France, but she chose not to. But would things have been different if she had?

Izumi had been sent by his company to an art auction in France. Takeshi, his boss, had suggested he take his wife along.

"No, I wouldn't feel right doing that," she'd said with feigned reluctance. "It's a business trip, after all."

But it was clear that she hadn't been the least bit interested. Had she planned to use his absence to sleep with Takeshi? Had Takeshi's offer been a ruse to cover up their affair? Izumi supposed he could check on that point, at least, the next time he saw Takeshi.

It was on the flight back from France that it happened. Just after take-off, two men, who looked Middle Eastern, pulled out guns that they had managed to smuggle aboard. There was a huge ruckus in the cabin, but as the guns were trained on the passengers, their screams became muffled sobs. Soon the cabin was completely quiet. It wasn't clear how many hijackers there were – some others had forced their way into the cockpit. And then came the announcement: the plane was turning south to Algiers. Not long afterwards, the flight plan was changed to include a stop in Barcelona.

"The women and children are getting off!" yelled one hijacker. A mixture of relieved voices, stifled wails and desperate gasps filled the cabin. The hijackers laughed as several women stood up to leave before the plane had even landed.

"You plan to flap your arms and fly home?" said one.

Across the aisle from Izumi sat an older couple. The husband was portly and dressed in casual holiday clothes. The wife, who looked much younger than her husband, was immaculately dressed.

"You have to go," said the husband.

"No, I'm not getting off this plane without you."

"Algiers is a dangerous place. I can survive by myself, but having you with me will put us both in danger. Please, you have to get off."

"No, I'm not going."

Izumi was deeply touched. The couple must have loved each other very much. What kind of people would be so devoted to one another? Many of the wives on board had decided to get off without any discussion and were busily preparing to leave. Izumi had no doubt that his wife wouldn't have hesitated.

The couple was none other than Nobuteru and his wife Nobuko, but Izumi had no way of knowing about his distant ties with them.

The plane landed in Barcelona, and as the women and children left the plane, Nobuteru tried to persuade his wife to go with them. She refused to leave her seat. A half-hour passed, and a hijacker noticed that Nobuko was still on board and ordered her to get off. "No!" Nobuko screamed in English and clung to her husband. The hijacker watched as Nobuteru pleaded with his wife to get off and she continued to shake her head. Finally the hijacker smiled and told them both to get off the plane. At first Nobuteru did not understand, but Nobuko immediately got up and pulled her husband to his feet.

As he walked towards the exit, Nobuteru turned to the hijacker and thanked him. The man smiled wryly, saying something that probably meant Nobuteru should be grateful for having such a good wife. After they had got off, one of the passengers cried out:

"Damn it! Some people have all the luck! My wife left without giving me a second glance!"

Laughter spread through the cabin. Izumi laughed as well. He had been so impressed he wanted to applaud as the couple left. The remaining passengers were mostly Japanese, nearly all middle-aged except for a few in their twenties and thirties; there were several Europeans as well, probably French. There were no elderly men left on board, so perhaps the hijackers would have let the couple go in any case.

The plane took off once again and headed south to Algiers with Izumi aboard.

The plane crashed not long afterwards. It was said that a hijacker fired his gun in the cockpit, but it was never clear precisely what happened. From that day on, Nobuteru felt deeply indebted to his wife. She had, after all, saved his life. They had been in love when they married, but after more than forty years he wasn't sure that she still loved him. The experience made his feelings for her grow strong once again.

Whenever they talked about the hijacking, Nobuko would say, "That was the second time I saved someone's life, you know."

Nobuko often told the story of how her younger brother Koichi had nearly been kidnapped when he was three years old. One day Nobuko, who was seven years older, noticed that Koichi wasn't in the house. She went out to look for him. Before long she met an old woman whom she had often seen while they walked their dogs.

"Have you seen my little brother? I can't find him anywhere," asked Nobuko, desperate.

The old woman seemed a bit surprised. "That was your little brother?"

Nobuko continued to look for Koichi as the old woman watched. Finally the woman called out:

"Wait here. I'll go look around where I saw him. If I find him, I'll bring him back."

The old woman walked towards the outskirts of the neighbourhood and came back ten minutes later with Koichi in tow. From what the family was able to piece together later, the old woman had offered Koichi sweets to get him to go with her. She then handed Koichi over to someone in exchange for cash. Such things often happened before the war. If Nobuko hadn't known the old woman from walking their dogs together, Koichi would have almost certainly been sold to a circus, or worse.

Hearing this story made Nobuteru feel close to Koichi. Of course Koichi was now a grown man working at the Tokyo Metropolitan Government Office and approaching retirement – hardly of an age when Nobuteru could shower him with affection. But Nobuteru always had a warm spot in his heart for him, and Koichi in turn always liked being with him and still called him "big brother". They often visited each other and went drinking together. It was a closeness that went beyond brothers-in-law.

One day Koichi invited Nobuteru to dinner at a small restaurant he'd never been to before. Nobuteru found Koichi waiting for him in a tiny private room.

"I know you have a great deal of experience in these matters," said Koichi after a bit. "And you helped me deal with those yakuza who showed up at the property administrative department a while back. So I wanted to ask your advice about a situation that has come up."

There was in Nobuteru's neighbourhood an ornate rococo-style home known as the Kashiwara Mansion that had been built in the 1920s. Its architecture was unusual for Japan, and it was often photographed for magazines and as a backdrop for television shows. When the owner of the house died, the heirs had been unable to pay the inheritance tax, and the government took possession of the property. The plan was to demolish the historic structure and put up a government building, but the residents in the area had started a campaign to save the mansion. Could Nobuteru help with this problem? asked Koichi. If so, he would be generously compensated.

Nobuteru decided to accept the job. It would allow him to stretch his dramatic skills, and his remuneration would be guaranteed. First, Nobuteru requested the names of the fifty-three people who had signed the petition to save the mansion. Next, he opened a bank account in the name of the Historic Kashiwara Mansion Preservation Fund using two million yen of his own money. He then proceeded to visit each of the signers in turn, his bankbook in hand.

"I want to save the old Kashiwara Mansion," he told the petitioners. "I've visited the government offices many times about this, and they've finally agreed to allow our organization to purchase the building and the surrounding two hundred and thirty square metres of land for the price of one hundred million yen. Of course, that's on the condition that we will be responsible for the repair, restoration and maintenance of the property, which I will be happy to pay for out of my own pocket. However, for the initial one hundred million yen, I must turn to the fifty-three of you who have been fighting to preserve this historic building. As you can see, I've donated two million yen myself. If each of the petitioners does the same, we'll have one hundred million yen. Can I count on your support? You will be made a member of the board of directors once the property has been made an official historic site."

Most of the people looked at Nobuteru as if he was insane, but that was exactly what he had expected. The only wrinkle in his plan occurred when an elderly woman by the name of Aya Naramoto obediently deposited two million yen in his account. Nobuteru did not want to be liable for fraud, so he quickly wrote her a receipt for the funds and signed a statement that if he was unable to raise the entire one hundred million yen, he would promptly return her money. While Nobuteru continued his fundraising efforts, men from the government demolition team periodically visited the mansion site. Seeing them poking around one day, members of the campaign called an emergency meeting, to which Nobuteru invited himself. He quickly assumed the role of the leader and began to bellow at the government representatives:

"I've already talked to you people about this! I was told that the demolition would not take place until the end of next month! We need time to raise the money! Don't tell me you haven't heard about that! Go get someone who knows what he's talking about! Go on, get out of here!"

The government representatives had been briefed by Koichi about the situation, and quickly left after Nobuteru's outburst. Nobuteru then used the opportunity to speak to the assembled group.

"Why haven't you donated to the preservation fund?" he cried. "Anyone living in a wealthy neighbourhood like this should be able to spare a measly two million yen! You say you want the building saved, but it's a different story if you have to cough up a little of your own money! Just think how proud you'll be to have a historic site like this in your own neighbourhood! But you just want to enjoy the benefits without taking any responsibility for it! I don't care what it takes! Each and every one of you is going to donate two million yen by the middle of next month! Do you hear me?"

Nobuteru grew increasingly manic as he spoke, and this continued when he visited the members' houses to ask for donations. He would show them the entry for Mrs Naramoto's two million yen in his bankbook and berate them for not following her example. And as Nobuteru had hoped, membership in the preservation campaign began to dwindle until there was only a small group lead by two intellectuals. This group advocated making the building an official historic site but had no interest in buying the property themselves. Convincing this group to give up required all of Nobuteru's skill. He visited each person repeatedly, almost to the point of harassment, and each time he would rave and blather on, his eyes red with passion. After a while Nobuteru could no longer tell if the madness he displayed was real or feigned.

Finally, the day of the demolition arrived. Nobuteru waited outside the Kashiwara Mansion from early that morning, but he was alone. No one from the group was there. His steady stream of vitriol had ensured that no one even came to witness the demolition, which took place without incident. As a finishing touch, he mugged in an appropriately exaggerated manner for the television cameras that had come to cover the event and then went directly to the bank to transfer Mrs Naramoto's two million yen back into her account. Koichi was very grateful, and when Nobuteru received his remuneration of four million five hundred thousand yen, the two of them went out to celebrate, and drank the night away.

Several days later, Nobuteru had a dream. He was standing in front of the Kashiwara Mansion. No, not precisely in front of it. The mansion was situated on a cliff and Nobuteru was standing on a path below it, looking up at the two-storey structure. No workers were in sight, but the structure was being slowly demolished. Sections of wall fell without a sound, until finally the entire building collapsed, taking the cliff with it. It all came rolling down towards Nobuteru in a dusty tidal wave of gravel, earth, tiles and bricks.

Nobuteru began to run. But he found that there were cliffs on either side of him and debris was pouring over them as well. Soon his path was almost completely covered, and he had to wade through the valley of rubble, pushing and kicking his way through. Suddenly, he was met with the mask-like faces of corpses poking out from the rubble. There had been a cemetery on the cliff, and it had collapsed in the landslide.

Even as he sweated and screamed in his nightmare, Nobuteru realized its source: in Sasayama, where Nobuteru and his family had fled to during the war, there had been a cemetery like this, where the dead were buried whole instead of being cremated. Children who dared to venture into the cemetery were so frightened that they wet themselves. Ominous dreams like this – dreams of meeting the dead – were best woken from as quickly as possible.

"Wake up!" he thought, and mustered all of his strength to force himself awake.

Could the nightmare have been caused by his guilt for having deceived the members of the preservation campaign? Surely a crafty old buzzard like Nobuteru was impervious to such feelings. And yet the episode had left a mark on his mind. He had begun to think about death almost obsessively. Perhaps the dream was a sign. Perhaps coming so close to the dead in his dream was an indication that he could cross over from his dreams into the next world if he should so desire.

I'm still dreaming, but where did Yuzo go?

Daté was sitting by himself in the middle of a traditional Japanese room. The sliding door behind him was closed, and there was an oblong brazier before him on which an iron kettle sat steaming. Parts of the room reminded him of his family's home out on the Yakihata Line, and yet it also seemed like a room in the house of the boss of the Sakaki gang. It seemed to him that he had been sitting there for a long time, but he did not know where he was. If you could really travel to Hell in a dream like Yuzo said, then maybe he had ended up in Hell. It wouldn't have surprised him, not after what he had been through.

Daté knew that he wasn't a real man – not like Yuzo was. Yuzo said that being orphaned during the war was what had made him grow up. But when Daté was that age he had still been in primary school. Once he had been playing with friends and fell and hit his knee. His friends gathered round him, worried about his injury, but when he started to cry and call out for his mother, they broke into laughter. Even through his tears, Daté saw the humour in the situation, and he began to laugh as well. But when he thought about it later, his feelings turned into embarrassment and then into unfocused rage. He had carried this rage with him into adulthood.

Things only got worse for him in junior high school. He was arrested for shoplifting and would often get into fights with other boys, sometimes seriously injuring them. He didn't throw away his junior-high-school graduation photo, though. In it, Daté was in the third row. Perhaps because his teacher disliked him, Daté had been given a small wobbly chair to stand on. He looked like a gasping goldfish as he struggled to make himself seen behind the tall boy in front of him and the heavy-set boys to either side. He managed a smile, but his expression was such a desperate attempt to assert his existence that Daté felt miserable every time he looked at the photo. He had saved it just because it was the only picture of a girl in his class he had a crush on. For all his skill at fighting, he was very shy around girls. Yes, thinking back, Daté realized what a baby he was then.

Yuzo had once told Daté about a dream he had while he was living on the streets of Tokyo as a war orphan. He was always hungry, which made him think of the Buddhist "Hell of starvation" his grandmother used to tell him about. In Yuzo's dream he went to Hell and ate a terrific feast. Yuzo said he remembered thinking that even Hell might be better than the life he was living.

You told me about that dream when I asked about what you wrote on the last page of your notebook. You know, the notebook you kept ever since you were a kid before the war. It might've been the last thing you ever wrote. It was funny, like a poem. I still remember it.

I dreamt I went to Hell
And had a giant feast.

"I wanted to write a poem about my dream," said Yuzo with a smile. "But I could only come up with those two lines. I guess I wasn't cut out to be a poet."

Yuzo and Takeshi were sitting on a bench on the roof of a department store. There were a variety of rides for children there, but there were few children and many old people in this world of the dead, and so they sat unused. The sky was clear and the air was dry.

"In that dream, were you taken to the restaurant by a couple of refined gentlemen?" asked Takeshi. "Or should I say a couple of refined-*looking* men?"

"Yes. How did you know that?"

"I was sitting at the next table."

Yuzo sat back in surprise. "Then I really did go to Hell. Amazing. I always thought that Hell was connected to the world of dreams." Yuzo looked at Takeshi, his face momentarily showing the same intensity it had in his previous life. "Then you saw how pitiful I was."

"That's right," said Takeshi. "But I think it was perfectly natural. After all, I know what it's like to be starving. I'm sure I would have done something similar. Those two men were from our generation. They must have had similar experiences. And yet they still treated you terribly. Trust me, they weren't trying to be nice to you. I'm sure they're still here, if you want to get back at them. What do you say we go to that restaurant one more time? We might see them."

"I don't care about revenge," said Yuzo, flashing his nihilistic smile once again. "Things like that don't mean anything to me any more. Besides, I'd never fit in at that kind of place anyway."

Yuzo had laughed when he told Takeshi about how he had been killed. What a ridiculous way to die, he said.

But what way of dying isn't ridiculous? thought Takeshi. Didn't everyone think that about their own death? People who achieved great things in their life probably thought at the moment of their death that everything they'd achieved was meaningless. When very rich people died, they were always deep in debt. And even people who live long lives must eventually think that going on living is pointless.

Takeshi didn't think this just because he wanted to feel better about his own death. Regardless of what he had thought before, now that he was dead it didn't really matter to him how he'd died.

In life, Takeshi had often found himself the object of a woman's affections; more than one or two had confessed her love for him. At first they felt sympathy for him, with his crippled legs and his crutches. Then they would notice his elegant manner and convince themselves that they had discovered a hidden quality in him that didn't exist in other men. Finally their hearts would be stolen by his good looks. They thought that he was special and that their love for him was unique.

There are ways of playing on a woman's sympathies, of steering her in a certain direction, of smoothing over the realities of adultery, and Takeshi learnt them all soon after his comparatively early puberty. The fact that he was indeed unique in some sense only served to heighten women's attraction to him. Innocent housewives were the most common, and in fact this type of woman appealed to Takeshi. It may have been that he subconsciously wanted revenge against their husbands because they were able-bodied or because they reminded him of the bullies he had to endure in school. But it had happened so many times, and with so many women, that to Takeshi the experience was anything but unique.

One evening, Takeshi was leaving a meeting with a client at a hotel when a child who had been running around the lobby knocked his crutches out from under him, causing him to fall and hit his hip against a large plant pot. A woman by the name of Motoko came running to help him up. She wasn't the child's mother. She was just a housewife who happened to be passing by. Takeshi gave her his business card and, having gained her trust by demonstrating his social standing, succeeded in getting her phone number. A week later, Takeshi invited her to dinner, saying that he wanted to thank her for her kindness. In addition to his thanks, he gave her small presents, and soon he was giving her expensive jewellery. Before two weeks had passed, they were sleeping together.

"I told my husband about you," she said one afternoon. Motoko was married to Daisaburo Shimada, the president of a small shipping company. The company had been experiencing financial difficulties; cutbacks had forced him to drive one of the company's dumper trucks himself. He had become suspicious after seeing his wife with jewellery that he could never afford, and so he followed her. When he confronted her, Motoko confessed her affair.

"I can't bear the thought of separating," she said to Takeshi. But it was not her marriage she was referring to, it was her relationship with Takeshi. When Takeshi realized this, he lost interest in her immediately. But already Motoko had made up her mind to leave her husband.

Takeshi received a call at his office from Daisaburo.

"She says she's in love with you. She wants to divorce me. Where is she?"

"I don't know where she is, but if I hear from her, I'll tell her to go home."

That had ended the matter for the moment, but a few days later Takeshi got a phone call from Motoko.

"I was staying with a friend," she said. "Daisaburo found me there and forced me to go with him." She no longer referred to him as her husband.

"Where are you now?"

"I'm at his house. I'm practically a prisoner here. I told him I still love you, but he won't give me a divorce."

On the day of his death, Takeshi had been in the company car on the way to the bank. Shortly after his driver pulled onto the motorway, Takeshi noticed a truck in the fast lane behind them hurtling towards them and warned his driver about it. A moment later, the truck slammed into them and the car was crushed, wedged between the truck and the guard rail of the highway.

Takeshi was killed instantly, and yet he found himself standing at the scene of the accident. He no longer needed his crutches. His driver was seriously injured; an ambulance sped away taking him to a hospital. Takeshi observed his own battered body lying on a stretcher as if it were someone else's. There was no doubt that he was dead. The driver of the truck, Daisaburo himself, was being questioned by the police, but Takeshi felt no anger. It seemed a certainty that Daisaburo would be arrested for homicide. Takeshi decided to move on. He nimbly jumped down from the thirty-foot-high motorway into the next world.

Being murdered would usually be considered an unfortunate way to die. But Takeshi had no reservations, no regrets. Once you were dead, you lost all feelings of attachment to the world of the living, and that made it impossible to wish your death had been any different. The only feelings he had were of amazement at how quickly and smoothly the transition had been made, and of joy at his immortal body, which had no need for crutches. But even these feelings soon dissipated.

Perhaps because he had frozen to death, Sasaki often wondered whether the traditional inferno version of Hell really existed. This was partly due to the story he had read, but it was also because he had met a number of people who seemed like they belonged in that kind of Hell. It wasn't that they had done anything bad enough to deserve being burned alive. It was just that, given how close his Hell was to the real world, a "burning inferno" could quite likely be nothing more than a place where you were forced to drink warm beer. Actually, considering that he had frozen to death, he wouldn't have minded that kind of Hell.

Sasaki had been walking along an avenue when he spotted a taxi idling at the kerb. Where would a taxi take people in Hell?

"Want a ride?" the portly middle-aged driver called out to Sasaki through the open taxi window.

"Where are you going?"

"No place special. Just for a drive. The scenery's different every time I take somebody for a drive here. I guess it changes dependin' on the passenger. Funny, huh?"

Sasaki got in. He had sensed that the driver had died in an accident, and he wanted to know his story.

"You were a taxi driver in the real world too, right?" asked Sasaki as soon as the car was in traffic. "How did you end up here?"

"Everybody asks me that," said the driver, laughing. "It's a pretty stupid story, but I'll tell you if you want to hear it. This really thin lady in a kimono gets into my cab. It's a really hot summer day. Now, you can probably tell just by lookin' at me, but I usually feel hot, so I had the air conditioning on full blast. But this lady, she says to me, 'Driver, I can't stand air conditioning. Please turn it off.' I guess there are a lot of people like that. I don't have any choice, so I turn the AC off. Soon the inside of the cab is like a Turkish bath. So I try openin' a window. 'Please close that window,' she says. Pretty soon the sweat is pourin' down my forehead and drippin' into my eyes and I can't see a thing in front of me. So I pull over to the side of the road and I say, 'Sorry, lady, but I'm sweatin' so much I can't see the road. I don't wanna cause an accident, so could you please get out here and find another cab?' 'What?' she says. 'I'll never catch another cab here. Can't you just take me a little further?' What could I do? I keep drivin'.

Finally, just when we're comin' to an intersection, the sweat in my eyes made 'em hurt so bad that I couldn't keep 'em open. So I say, 'I'm sorry, lady, but you see that signal up ahead? Is it red, or is it green?' Then she gets all flustered. 'What? The signal? Uh, um… It's red. No, it's green,' she says. When she says it's green, I pull out into the intersection and *wham*, we get sideswiped by a truck. My cab went flying. Me and the lady were crushed. We died instantly. Funny how things work out."

"I wonder why you were sent here. Did the woman come here, too?"

"I haven't seen her. Maybe she's somewhere else."

Who was in charge of who went to Hell and who didn't? It couldn't just be random, could it? This wouldn't be the only time that Sasaki would wonder about this.

Although he had insisted to Takeshi that he wasn't interested in going to the restaurant from his dream, Yuzo ended up going there alone. He had wanted to check that it had actually been real, but he didn't feel like going there with Takeshi. He entered the familiar-looking restaurant and sat at what seemed to be the same table he'd sat at as a child. He was looking around, doing his best to quell the feelings of embarrassment that this environment threatened to rekindle, when the same expressionless, proper-looking waiter came to take his order.

"Do you remember me?" Yuzo asked.

The waiter studied Yuzo carefully and smiled. "So you were that little street urchin?"

"That's right. I was starving."

"I understand." The waiter nodded deeply. "Surely you're not ashamed of how you acted?"

"No. That's why I was able to come here today."

"Well, you're most welcome."

He seemed to be sincere. Still, Yuzo had no intention of opening up to him.

The waiter went on, "Yes, most welcome indeed."

"Do those two men come here often?"

"That's hard to say," said the waiter, an uncomfortable look coming over his face. "One loses all track of time here. But I imagine you've noticed that already." He hurriedly added, "I do know that you came here quite early."

He seemed to mean that Yuzo had died at an early age. Yuzo guessed that Takeshi was actually much older than he had looked. That is, his true form must have been older, but somehow he was able to change his appearance depending on whom he was with. Or maybe he only appeared that way to Yuzo. Yuzo, on the other hand, seemed to have only one immortal form. His fellow gang members would definitely recognize him if they saw him there. What could Daté and Hattori be up to now? They would surely be coming to Hell when they died, so they must not have been killed yet. He felt sorry for them; he had put them through a lot.

On opening night at the Kabukiza Theatre, before he was to walk down the elevated runway that extended into the audience, Konzo Ichikawa got lost in the storage area under the stage. It should have been a short detour to the little curtained waiting room where he would await his cue, but someone had rearranged the props kept there, turning the area into a veritable labyrinth.

Even in his bewildered state, Konzo realized that

this had to be the work of Yamatoya. The part of Iso no Toyata was a speciality of Yamatoya's, and it must have been a terrible blow that it should go to the likes of Konzo, who was not a member of a famous kabuki family. But in fact the theatrical company had included the play in the roster specifically so that the popular and talented Konzo could play the part.

Konzo hit his knee against a prop boulder and moaned. Onstage above him, Narikomaya and Monzaburo had only a few minutes of drawn-out dialogue before Konzo was to make his entrance.

"But do I really have the right to ask for Shinobu's life, even to save my own?" The voice was that of Yamatoya's son Monzaburo, who played the parts of Kyonokimi and her servant Shinobu, who was to be sacrificed in her place.

Now that Konzo thought about it, Narikomaya had been quite nasty during rehearsals, making snide remarks about the kind of people who would stoop to appear on television. But Konzo didn't have time to think about that now. He had to hurry and find his way.

Konzo had on a *haori* coat; he was wearing a black

wig and his face was painted with circles of dark crimson around his eyes. A gourd dangled from the cherry branch slung over his shoulder. This light-hearted new role was certain to make Konzo even more popular, and he wasn't about to let Yamatoya ruin it for him.

But in the dimness of the storage area, the only light coming from emergency lamps, Konzo struggled to regain his sense of direction. He was lost. He felt around with his hands and feet, straining to find his way. He would take off in one direction and trip over something, then turn back and run into something else.

"You must consider your position, as well as the life of the unborn child in your womb," Narikomaya was now saying.

"And yet that is little more than an excuse," replied Monzaburo in a shrill falsetto. "If it were not for Benkei's compassion, I would already be dead. Alas, Shinobu must die if I am to live…"

Konzo's mouth suddenly dropped open. They were all in on it, he realized. Of course. That fox-faced Monzaburo had been smirking at him ever since the first rehearsal; he and Narikomaya had been whispering and laughing to each other. They had been planning this even then. But the mastermind behind it all was certainly Yamatoya. Only a star of his stature could have engineered a grand scheme like this. He even had the stagehands working for him. Konzo's servant Kunihiro was supposed to have been here to escort him to the waiting room by the stage, but at the last minute he had been reassigned to prop duty. Yamatoya had been behind that too. But there was nothing he could do about it now. His cue was coming up, and he was going to miss it.

NARIKOMAYA: "If you are to live, you must accept Shinobu's sacrifice and dedicate your life to serving Buddha in atonement for what must be done. Ironic, is it not, that she should be named Shinobu?"

MONZABURO: "Shinobu. To withdraw from the world. And that is what I must do."

NARIKOMAYA: "An inauspicious name indeed."

From behind the curtains, SOMEONE cries out: "Toyata has returned!"

Konzo threw his head back in frustration. They had gone right ahead without checking if he was present. If an actor wasn't ready in the wings before he was to go onstage, someone was supposed to go find him. Damn. Everyone was a part of the conspiracy! He started walking again, only to trip on a prop *jizo* statue and fall to the floor. Damn! His costume was now covered in dust and getting soaked in sweat. He couldn't go onstage like this! Above him, Narikomaya and Monzaburo continued reciting their lines to one another. They seemed quite cheerful – because they knew he was trapped.

NARIKOMAYA: "What's that? Toyata has returned?"

MONZABURO: "Then until the deed is done…"

NARIKOMAYA: "We must keep what we spoke of today…"

MONZABURO and NARIKOMAYA (*in unison*): "…a secret."

(*Pause.*)

MONZABURO and NARIKOMAYA (*in unison*): "Welcome home, Toyata!"

(*Enter Toyata with a cough.*)

That was Konzo's direction. What was he going to do? He could at least manage the cough.

"*Ahem!*"

Could they hear him? He ploughed his way through a prop bush, only to bump against the wall of the machine room. Damn. He had been going round in circles. That rotten stagehand. He was the one who had done this. Konzo was directly under the centre of the stage now. He hurriedly turned back again, determined not to be fooled this time by the maze of props around him, and proceeded straight ahead in what he thought was the direction to the stairway leading to the stage entrance. He could hear Narikomaya and Monzaburo onstage chuckling to one another.

NARIKOMAYA: "Oh dear, Shinobu. I have heard that Toyata had returned and yet I see no sign of him."

MONZABURO: "Whatever could have happened to Toyata?"

NARIKOMAYA: "He's been appearing on television quite often recently. Perhaps he's still there?"

The audience laughed. Konzo was frantic and tripped on another prop, which sent him to the floor, flat on his face. Unable to bear it any longer, he cried out in a voice so loud he felt his throat might split from the force of it.

"Here I am! I'm down here! Please make my apologies to your mother, Shinobu!"

MONZABURO: "Where could that voice be coming from?"

NARIKOMAYA: "It seems to be coming from the ground."

MONZABURO: "Yes, it is definitely coming from the ground."

NARIKOMAYA: "From the depths of Hell, perhaps."

MONZABURO: "That faint voice. It could be none other than…"

MONZABURO and NARIKOMAYA (*in unison*): "Konzo Ichikawa!"

Konzo jumped in fury. How far were they willing to take this? He would not let them make him into a laughing stock! He started running like a scared rabbit, collided with another prop, and tumbled to the floor again. Holding one leg in pain, he hopped towards the dim light he saw before him. Surely that was the stairway.

As he reached the spot, he recognized the set for Iwa Daimyojin Temple, in which he had performed *Ghost Story at Yotsuya on the Tokaido*. It was decorated with red streamers, and light bulbs shone dimly in the votive candle-holders on either side.

"Why have you cursed me, Iwa-*sama*? I have done nothing wrong. Please forgive me if I have. Save me from this torment!" pleaded Konzo, scraping and bowing, his hands clasped together, before finally bursting into tears. Onstage above him, the repartee of the actors went on:

MONZABURO: "He let his meagre talents go to his head and he started bragging about how popular he was."

NARIKOMAYA: "The vile Konzo even had the nerve to poke fun at kabuki itself."

MONZABURO: "Even now, he is no doubt spouting jokes at our expense somewhere, regardless of the rules of our profession."

KONZO: "No—o! That's not true! I'm right here! I'll be there soon!"

Konzo stood up to see a statue of the deity Inari, flanked by two foxes. "Damn that Monzaburo. Damn him to Hell."

Konzo's eyes were blank as he stared out into the darkness. He had begun to whisper to himself, reciting his lines as if to keep from forgetting them. But this soon degenerated into delirious babbling.

"I'm not conceited, really I'm not. I only told those jokes because I was on television. That's all. Iwa-*sama*! Inari-*sama*! Please make them stop!"

Where was he now? He had walked and walked and yet the storage area never seemed to end. But now as he looked around, he didn't seem to be in the storage area at all. It was some sort of basement room. He wasn't under the stage. Could he be under the building next door? But there were baskets, paper lanterns and other props scattered about, so he had to be in the Kabukiza. He heard a noise coming through a small grated window. It was the painfully familiar sound of an underground train approaching and then receding. He pressed his ear to the window and wept.

"Oh, blessed Inari," Konzo prayed. "They say the worst things happen to the best people. Is that why this is happening to me? What have I done to deserve this? Was I conceited to go on television? Is that it? I was just trying to entertain people. That's all. But I didn't ignore my rehearsals. And I went and greeted all the guests on opening night, just as I was supposed to. Please, I'll do anything. Just forgive me!"

As they sat in the Night Walker, the cast of *Premiere 21* could talk of nothing but how Konzo Ichikawa had disappeared under the stage of the Kabukiza. Izumi had been negotiating a deal with a businessman named Sasaki and arrived at the club later than usual. Yumiko saw him cutting straight across the dance floor and motioned to him, pointing to the empty seat beside her. Izumi came and sat down. He was one of them now. Kashiwazaki, Osanai and Shibata grinned at one another. They knew he was Yumiko's slave. But Yumiko herself couldn't have cared less what they thought, and in any case she was much more interested in the fate of Konzo Ichikawa.

"I heard that it was a plot by the other actors," said Yumiko breathlessly, continuing where she had left off before Izumi's arrival. "When a kabuki actor gets popular and goes on television, the other actors don't like it and they may him pay."

"But how could he go in there and not come out?" asked Kashiwazaki, knitting his brows at the thought. "It's been days."

"He must've croaked – I mean, passed away – by now. Don't you think?" said Shibata in a low voice, doing her best to hide her pleasure. Hearing about someone dying always made her feel strangely cheerful.

Kashiwazaki glared at Shibata. "What is it with you?" he asked, curling his lips. "Look at what you're wearing tonight: a bright red suit. Have a little respect."

"You know, I heard that they can still hear his voice from under the stage," said Nishizawa softly, trying to scare Kashiwazaki. "They've searched and searched, and they can't find any trace of him, but they say that when you stand on the stage you can faintly hear him reciting his lines."

"Oh God, no. No no no." Kashiwazaki began to shake. "I'm going to have nightmares about this."

"He must be haunting the place," said Osanai. "After all, he was a star on his way up. He must still have attachments to the world of the living."

"Excuse me, but do we really know that Konzo is dead?" said Izumi timidly. He had heard about the case in the news. "He's only been missing seven days. He could still be alive, even without anything to eat or drink. There are many cases of people surviving that long. Maybe he just got stuck somewhere."

"That's right," said Yumiko. "Believe me, I know what it's like under the stage at Kabukiza. I've been down there. It's terrible, a mess. The manager told me people get lost there all the time."

"Konzo Ichikawa, the doomed kabuki actor, wandering beneath the stage like a ghost..." said Nishizawa spookily.

"And today is the seventh day since his disappearance. His ghost might even show up here to haunt us..." said Osanai, joining in.

"Boo!" shouted Yumiko, suddenly tapping Kashiwazaki on the back. He fainted, hitting the table with enough force to knock off glasses and dishes.

Konzo continued to wander. The room seemed to go on for ever. Could the basements of all the buildings in the world be connected? The area beneath the Kabukiza stage was one storey below ground – an area elsewhere taken up by underground shopping plazas. But here there was only a single dreary, cold, concrete corridor lit by dim emergency lamps. There was no sign of human life. Where was he? He was no longer in the world he had known – that much was clear – and yet he had no recollection of dying. Was this a dusky creation of his consciousness? Was he trapped in a twilight figment of his imagination?

In the distance he could see a vertical strip of light. What was it? And what were those muffled sounds of life that seemed to be coming from that direction? Shaking now, Konzo hauled his tired frame onwards, drawn by the light and the voices.

He came to a door. What could be on the other side? Was it Hell? Konzo began to tremble. Did he have any other choice but to go in? His situation couldn't get any worse. He was as good as dead already. If there was a party going on, he would welcome it, even in the filthy state he was in.

It was a metal door – the kind you would find in a machine room. The steel handle was cold. He pushed down hard on it and pulled the door open. He was met with laughter, squeals, the clinking of glasses, the smell of steak and perfume. It was the Night Walker.

Mayumi Shibata and the novelist Yoshio Torikai had just left their hotel room when they were accosted outside the lift by two men, one of them holding a camera.

"I see you two just came out of that room," said the shorter man. He was buck-toothed and spat as he talked.

"Who are you?" demanded Torikai, who took great pride in being a novelist. He was not your garden-variety celebrity and he would not stand to be treated like one. But right now, he was trying his best to shield Shibata from the lens of the muscular man with a camera. Shibata's teeth were chattering as she hid behind Torikai's back.

"Ha ha ha. I'm a reporter. But you didn't really need me to tell you that, did you?" said the short man. "How long has this been going on?"

"If you're trying to get a story out of us," said

Torikai, pressing the lift button, "then you'll have to make an appointment."

"Oh, come on," laughed the reporter. "I don't think you understand the situation. Let's see here..." He looked over Torikai's shoulder at Shibata. "You were a guest on *Premiere 21*, weren't you? Is that when it all started?"

"I'll tell you all about it if you'll just make an appointment. I'll tell you anything you want to know."

"You're a married man, aren't you? So that makes this, you know, adultery."

"I told you to make an appointment!" shouted Torikai. "What are you, a moron?!" He tried to get away from the small man, but the photographer kept trying to get a photo of Shibata.

Anger flashed briefly on the reporter's face, but he quickly regained his composure. "Shall I just say you didn't deny anything?"

"I told you I'd tell you everything, didn't I? My God, your breath stinks."

The lift doors opened. Fortunately it was empty, and Torikai and Shibata scurried in. "Stay away from us. I can't stand the stench," Torikai shouted, as he pushed the reporter and photographer out of the lift.

"I guess I'll just have to say you panicked and ran away!" the reporter shouted back.

Shibata burst into tears as soon as the doors closed, and Torikai pulled her to him. "If Bungei owns the tabloid," he said, "I can try to hush it up."

"When do you think it'll be published?"

"Within the next couple of weeks maybe."

"Your poor wife."

Torikai decided to put on hold telling his wife. After all, the article might not come out at all. But he had to face the fact that it was going to be published. He couldn't stop it. He just wasn't a big enough name in the publishing world. And once it was out, he was going to be put through Hell. Salvaging his marriage could take an eternity, and during that time he wouldn't be able to write. But writing was all he had! He loved his wife, but if they had to get divorced, so be it. He had been prepared for that possibility the first time he slept with Shibata. Or at least he thought he was prepared.

117

* * *

Mamoru Kashiwazaki felt like he was in Hell. He wasn't going to get paid for his next two concerts. His manager Osanai had been in charge of producing the concerts, but he had run off with the advance, leaving Kashiwazaki with nothing. Why had he trusted a man like that? In the industry they say the best managers do the worst things, and Osanai had been a very good manager.

Of course, managers who ripped off their clients always found their way back into the business. Sooner or later they turned up managing someone else as if nothing ever happened.

Kashiwazaki tossed and turned in bed. Ever since that evening at the Night Walker, he felt like he was cursed. He had never been so scared. He had been there with the usual group from *Premiere 21*. Konzo's disappearance was already old news, but for some reason Kashiwazaki couldn't help staring at the place on the sofa where Konzo had always sat. Everyone seemed down. Mayumi Shibata was especially depressed because hints of her affair with Yoshio Torikai had come out in the tabloids.

"Come on, snap out of it," said Osanai. He hadn't yet run off with Kashiwazaki's cash, but he must have been planning it. "If you really want to be an actress, you've got to get used to things like this. If you want to have a private life, forget about television. Maybe you should try stage acting."

"Wait a minute," said Nishizawa quickly. "We plan to have her on the show for a long time. Don't put ideas into her head."

Nishizawa was also depressed. His wife, he discovered, had borrowed heavily from a loan shark to pay for her Louis Vuitton bags and Chanel suits, and he was now struggling to make the outrageous loan payments. "These guys just won't give up," he said. "They call me every day with their thick Osaka accents. 'You think you can mess with us? We'll sell your wife to a whorehouse! You don't know who you're dealin' with!' The other day they came to the TV station and hassled the security guards. Don't they realize that I'll never be able to pay them back if I lose my job?"

"It really does sound like you don't know who you're dealing with," said Yumiko, who had once done a special report on loan sharks.

"I'm so sick of this," said Nishizawa. "I'm afraid to go home because I know they'll be waiting by the front door when I get there."

"Well, they don't seem to be here, at least," replied Yumiko, who began looking anxiously around the room. "You know," she said, "I could use a little compassion myself. I'm the one being stalked. The guy first showed up at a meeting of my fan club. Everything was going great, everybody laughing and having a good time, people lining up to introduce themselves to me. They even applauded every time I finished talking. But there was this one guy just standing in the corner, smiling creepily and not saying anything.

"Then he showed up a month later. I was eating breakfast with my husband, and he just walks right in and says, 'Good morning, Yumiko.' I probably forgot to lock the door when I took the rubbish out. Anyway, my husband yells, 'Who the hell are you?' The nutcase just laughs and says, 'That's what I was going to say to you!' Then he comes up to me and says, 'You always look so pretty, Yumiko. Come on, let's have breakfast.' I must've turned pale as a ghost. And then he sits right down at the table! My husband grabbed him by the neck and threw him out. The guy didn't put up a fight, but the whole time he was saying, 'What're you doing? *I'm* Yumiko's husband! Get your hands off me!'

"Since then, he's been showing up every couple of days. It doesn't matter what time it is or whether my husband is around or not. If I'm not there, he'll just wait for me by the front door. I went to the police, but they just laughed. They said a TV personality should expect this kind of thing. They found out his name, but because he hasn't hurt me and doesn't carry a weapon, the police think he's harmless. And they think he's mentally ill, so they won't arrest him because they're afraid some mental-illness advocacy group will make trouble for them.

"So now that he knows the police aren't going to touch him, he's got bolder and bolder, and he's been looking more and more disturbed. He waits for me at the television station. Sometimes he'll yell stuff at my husband and me. I'm afraid he'll come after us with a knife or something. I'm just so sick of it. I wish somebody would help me."

At that moment, Mamoru Kashiwazaki was frozen in fear. Konzo Ichikawa, still in his stage make-up and kimono, was coming slowly towards him. He came not from the direction of the dance floor, but rather from a passageway between the box seats. He was floating just above the floor, reaching out with both arms towards his friends, smiling sadly, as if asking them to take him back into the group.

Kashiwazaki's eyes grew large. He stared at Konzo, his lips quivering, unable to speak or move, paralysed with fear. But none of the others noticed. Yumiko continued her tale of woe. Finally, Kashiwazaki fainted, falling face down onto the table.

"Here we go again," said Osanai, annoyed.

"Lay him down and put his feet up," said Nishizawa, who then began to tend to Kashiwazaki. Several patrons stood around, watching.

As soon as he regained consciousness, Kashiwazaki

looked at the faces peering down at him. "Is he here? Is he? Is he? Is he?" he mumbled.

"Who?"

"Konzo... Konzo... Konzo Ichikawa."

"Of course he's not here," said Yumiko. "You saw something, didn't you? What did you see?"

"He was coming from over there," said Kashiwazaki, pointing towards the passageway, at the end of which was the steel emergency-exit door.

"You must have just imagined it," said Yumiko, stroking Kashiwazaki's long hair. "You know how overworked you get."

"Is he all right?" asked an expressionless waiter who had approached the table.

Still shaking, Kashiwazaki sat up. "I wasn't imagining it," he said. "You really didn't see him? No one did? Well I know what I saw. Wait, what happened to Izumi? He didn't see him too, did he? Where's Izumi? Where did he go?"

"Don't get so excited," said Yumiko, pressing gently down on Kashiwazaki's shoulders to keep him from sitting up. "Izumi isn't here today."

"That's not true. I saw him there. Right next to you."

"He went to France on business," said Osanai. "Remember he talked about it? He had to go to that auction in Paris."

Nishizawa had been called away for a phone call, and his face was grim as he returned. "That was the TV station," he reported. "They just got the news of a hijacked flight from Paris. They said there was someone named Izumi among the Japanese passengers. And... they said that the plane crashed."

"*Aaaaggghhh!*" Kashiwazaki jumped up with a shriek.

That was the last time that anyone in the group went to the Night Walker. But Kashiwazaki still dreamt of talking with his friends there, at the club with the sprawling dance floor. In his dreams, the place was always warm and filled with the aromas of food. Both Konzo Ichikawa and Yoshitomo Izumi were there. Konzo with the same make-up and stage costume as the night Kashiwazaki had seen him, and Izumi in his usual spot next to Yumiko.

Kashiwazaki couldn't sleep. He was afraid to. He tossed and turned. He couldn't avoid sleep for ever. He was in Hell when he was awake and in Hell when he was asleep. It was like all the little hells he had endured since childhood had joined together to torment him as an adult. He had been called a "pansy" in junior high, and he was called a "queer" in high school. Yes, his life had been Hell. The promoters said that they wouldn't pay him – his manager already got his cut – but they would pay his band, which meant that he had a rehearsal the next day. He didn't have any choice. People said that the promoters were yakuza, so what could he do? He had taken out a huge loan to buy his new luxury apartment, and now this...

Sachiko Izumi still lived in the house that her husband had bought. Her lover had died five years after the death of her husband, and more than twenty years had passed since then, but Sachiko still dreamt of them both. Mostly she dreamt of Takeshi.

She was asleep on the second floor when the doorbell rang. She got up and stepped out onto the landing in her white negligee. The door opened without a sound, and Takeshi walked in. For some reason, he didn't have his crutches with him.

As he removed his coat, Takeshi spoke matter-of-factly to Sachiko, paying no attention to her nervousness. "It's been a long time since we met that day at the hotel, hasn't it? We slipped away from your husband and went into the garden. I still think it's amazing how well we understood each another, considering we'd never met before."

Takeshi hung his coat on the rack before climbing the stairs. Was this reality or a dream?

"Oh, Takeshi. This is a dream, isn't it? You've been dead for over twenty years. You died in a traffic accident. Or maybe it was murder? Well, they called it an accident. This is a dream, isn't it? You've been dead for over twenty years now…"

"This isn't a dream, Sachiko."

Takeshi was already naked, already inside her. If it wasn't a dream, what was it? Reality? Despite her confusion, Sachiko soon succumbed to Takeshi's sensual skills and began to moan.

"Oh… My husband. My husband. He's… He's on

a business trip overseas. At an auction in Paris. No, that's not right. He died on his way back home. But how is that possible? It could only feel this good if he was alive. Yes, he is alive. He's just come home. He just walked in the front door. He's coming up the stairs."

"I know."

"He's coming up the stairs."

"I know."

"But how? How do you know?"

"This has happened before. So many times."

Of course. It might be a dream, but it wasn't the first time she had dreamt this. Didn't she have this dream night after night? Takeshi would not let Sachiko go. Her husband stood outside the partially opened bedroom door, and still he would not let her go. Now her husband was inside the bedroom, watching them.

"Yes. I've been through this so many times," said Izumi as he sat on the edge of the bed. "But I wasn't dreaming."

"Hello, Izumi."

"Hello, sir."

The two of them spoke as if they had seen each other only moments before. But they were both dead. They had been dead for so very long.

"You mean you two…" Sachiko pulled the sheets up to cover her body. "You two became friends… over there? In the other world?"

"Friends?" repeated Takeshi.

The two men exchanged faint smiles.

"Then this must be a dream, right? I'm in my bedroom dreaming that I'm in my bedroom. Right?"

"Sachiko. This isn't a dream."

"Then is it reality?"

"No. It's not reality," said Izumi brusquely.

If it wasn't a dream and it wasn't reality, what was it?

Sachiko raised her voice. "Then this must be Hell. It's not a dream. It's not reality. But I'm not dead. I'm alive but I can't go out of this bedroom. I can't go anywhere. I can't see anyone but you. That's Hell for me. This is my Hell."

Sachiko woke up. The doorbell was ringing. She went out onto the landing. She must have been dreaming before. The front door opened silently and Takeshi walked inside. As he took off his coat, he spoke matter-of-factly to Sachiko.

"It's been a long time since we met that day at the hotel, hasn't it? We slipped away from your husband and went into the garden. I still think it's amazing how well we understood one another, considering we'd never met before."

Takeshi hung his coat on the rack before climbing the stairs.

Sachiko began to question him. "This isn't a dream and it isn't reality. Then am I dead? If I was alive I should be an old woman."

"No, you're not dead," said Takeshi as he embraced Sachiko in her bed. "You'll live to be an old woman. You won't die for many years, and we will meet each other every night. And even after you die, you will be able to see me, your husband, and many other interesting people besides."

Time in Hell is not a constant. Three days in Hell might equal ten years in the real world. One can go back in time as well as see into the future. It was at some point in this indistinct flow of time that two old women happened upon one another in a town shrouded in mist. Or perhaps it was the smoke of an incinerator – the air was so hazy they couldn't see more than a few feet in front of them. One of the women was Sachiko, Izumi's wife. The other was Motoko, the wife of Daisaburo Shimada. As they passed one another on the pavement, they stopped and cocked their heads quizzically to one side. It seemed that their pasts were connected in some way. Were they distant relations? Or had one of them had an affair with the other's husband? The two women stared at each other for some time, and then they both realized the truth at the same instant. They had each had an affair with the same man. A look of mild surprise came across their faces, and then they walked away from each other with nothing more than a smile and a nod.

Sasaki was in his makeshift tent of plastic sheeting, trying to sleep in the bitter cold. No, no one could sleep in cold like this. The most he could manage was a light doze. He was talking with his wife Jitsuko, venting his anger at being fired over the kickback.

"Damn that Shinoda, damn that Shinoda…" he kept muttering.

His wife did her best to placate him. "I told you to stop thinking about it. Hate doesn't solve anything."

"And I had to drag you with me."

"Who else would have an ugly woman like me? Where can an old woman like me go?"

"It's cold."

"Yes."

"I feel terrible. My body's like ice. Do you think this is what it's like in the 'eight freezing hells'? We're going to die tonight. I just know it."

"Don't be silly. Soon the sun will come out and warm us up, just like it always does. This spot gets the most sun in the entire park."

After a while, his wife seemed to fall asleep beside him. From outside the tent came a man's voice.

"Mr Sasaki! Mr Sasaki!"

"Who is it? Who's there?"

"It's me, Izumi."

"What do you want? I heard you were dead." Was Sasaki dreaming? Could Izumi really be there? Sasaki sat up and looked through the plastic sheeting. He could see nothing more than a black silhouette. It could have been anyone. But there was no question that the voice was Izumi's.

"I came to apologize for what I did. For my part in putting you in your current circumstances."

Damn right, it was his fault. Sasaki didn't care if Izumi was a ghost. He'd teach him a thing or two. But all he could manage were a few lame insults: "So you decided to come back and apologize now that you're dead, eh? That sounds like something out of a kabuki play. I don't remember you talking like that while you were alive!"

"When you die, you lose all feelings of anger and hatred. That's why I came to apologize to you while you were still alive." The utter lack of emotion in Izumi's voice made it difficult for Sasaki to believe what he was saying. "Please, rail against me while you still can."

"You're talking like I'm going to die any minute now."

"I'm afraid that's true. I could meet you after your death, but then neither of us would be satisfied.

Please hurry. You will soon fall into a sleep from which you will never awaken."
Sasaki was walking in a park in broad daylight when he finally ran into Izumi again. It was not the park in which he and his wife had died; this park was in Hell. As the two men stood staring dumbly at one another, Sasaki finally understood what his dream had meant. Izumi really had visited him from Hell that night. And just as Izumi had said, now that Sasaki was dead, he was incapable of experiencing feelings of anger or hatred. And for that he was grateful.

Daté followed the big black dog down towards the river. The dog was running among the reeds when it seemed to stand up, and suddenly it was Yuzo, standing with his back to the setting sun.

Was that big black dog you, Yuzo? I'm sorry. I didn't know. I slept with my arms around you. Thanks for being in my dreams so many times. Yuzo... They killed you, didn't they? You're dead, right? So what about me? If I'm seeing you, then this must be a dream. Is that it? Or am I dead too?

"You idiot, this is no dream."

The voice was clear, not muffled, not an echo. It was the voice of the real Yuzo – the voice Daté remembered. And unlike in his previous dream, Yuzo was now smiling kindly at him. "And you're not dead either," the voice of Yuzo said. "You saw me getting killed and then you ran. Don't you remember? No, you're not dead. And neither is Hattori. In fact, we can go see him if you want."

The burly *mama-san* in her kimono was still torturing Hattori. Asahina and his men were lying on the sofa exhausted, watching the madness unfolding in front of them. She had taken back the knife that she had loaned Asahina and was waving it at Hattori as she spat curses at him in the dim reddish light of the bar. Her hair had come undone and hung down before her face. As she taunted Hattori, her eyes would roll up under their lids, revealing only the whites. Her mouth, smeared with lipstick, looked like the gaping cuff of a kimono sleeve.

"You men! You're all the same! You and your striped socks! It took me five years of slaving away to save three million five hundred thousand yen, but you thought nothing of stealing my bankbook and gambling it all away on horses and mah-jong! You just left me to keep on slaving here in this stinking sewer. And you said you worked for Mitsubishi! Ha! I can still see that smug look on your face, you lousy bastard!" she screamed, slapping Hattori's back with the flat of the knife.

The pain caused Hattori, still tied to the chair, to flinch away and howl. In his agony, he once again began to babble: "It hurts. It hurts. The poor burnt muscles on my back, my back! Is the fat back there white? Is it white? Does it look like sushi? Give me water! I need some water! What kind of sushi restaurant doesn't have water? Is the train about to leave? Is it going to my village? I hear the mosquitoes *buzzing buzzing buzzing* waiting for me to die..."

"You're all the same! You say you're the founder of a new religion, but you prey on people's insecurities so they hand over their savings! 'You've sinned a great deal,' you say. 'You must buy this urn to cleanse yourself,' you say. 'One million yen is a cheap price for eternal salvation.' And I had to go and sell my grandmother's house. I gave you the deed and then you went to the bathroom and you never came back!"

"It hurts. It hurts. I can't stand it any more, Miki! Come here, Miki! Come here come here come here! Why do you keep your sweet treasure all locked up like that? I won't give you any more presents until you let me die die die. Someone still wants to eat that shrimp so just let the dragonfly fly fly fly in the sky sky sky…"

"You had the nerve to call me an old bag! You with your stinking oily hair! You fucked the girls I worked so hard to find, my sweet pretty girls, my hostesses, you fucked every one of them! Shit shit shit! You got them pregnant, and still you showed up, night after night! Even after I changed bars, you followed me! That's all your kind cares about: fucking! You even tried to seduce *me*, you pig! I hope you die in the gutter!"

"It hurts. It hurts. I'm gonna die die die! I'm gonna die! Everything's red, but I see something black coming. Is it a person? A human being? A black man? Who is it? Who is it? I need water. Red water. Black water. My throat is burning. It's splitting open.

They're eating me. The demons are eating my arms and my legs and they're laughing. Laughing. It's so cold cold cold in this hole hole hole…"

"You college boys think you can do anything just because you're young and smart. You ask me up to your dirty filthy little apartment and like a fool I walk right in. And then you call me an old bitch, and before I know it I'm down on that dirty tatami mat. You and your five filthy friends think just because I'm old and ugly you can do anything you want to me. I can still smell your stinking breath as you took turns sticking your disgusting filthy pricks in me over and over…"

"It hurts. It hurts. It stings. Stings. Sings? We used to sing. We'd go to karaoke at that dingy little place in Yokohama with the stained yellow walls, but I guess I'll never go there again. It's all so pointless. Everything I did was meaningless. It's all over. All over."

"I was nineteen – or was it eighteen? You took an innocent country girl and made her think you loved her. You showed me your luxurious living room and then we went out onto the grass and I was so overwhelmed. I believed everything you said. We did it right there on the ground by the stone lanterns. And when we were done you said how rich your father was and how you could never marry someone poor and ugly like me! All the time you had a rich fiancée with a grand piano. Do you know how much I cried? How I thought about killing myself? How I, I…"

This time the flat of the knife hit one of Hattori's open wounds, plunging into his flesh. His body went stiff. The whites of his eyes turned up and his tongue flopped out of his mouth. The *mama-san* and the three gangsters jumped. Had she finally killed him? Was he dead? Hattori's body was slumped forwards, limp and lifeless.

But he quickly came to, sitting up, babbling even faster than before: "It hurts. It hurts. The quick brown fox jumps over the lazy dog. There's no time, Mr Tortoise, we'll be late for the goldfish's funeral. Miki-*chan*, are we still together? We were going to go to the beach at Atami, but not any more. The air in my lungs feels like needles, needles… Needless to say we're in Hell…"

138

* * *

Ten minutes after the plane left Barcelona, a shot was heard from behind the curtain by the cockpit. A second shot. Then a third. The plane shook violently. From where Izumi was sitting, there was no way to know whether the hijackers had shot the pilot, or if the pilot and the hijacker were fighting it out. Surely they hadn't shot both the pilot and co-pilot!

The two hijackers in the cabin took off towards the cockpit. A stewardess dashed from the cockpit, her face pale. The plane continued to shake, dropping noticeably. The cabin was in chaos. Izumi was desperate to know what was happening, wanting to prepare himself for what was coming.

Another stewardess ran towards the cockpit. As there were no hijackers in sight, passengers stood and began to shout questions at her.

"What happened?"

"Is the pilot all right?"

"Why are we shaking like this?"

"Are we going to crash? Are we going to crash?"

"Please stay in your seats with your seat belts

fastened." It seemed to be the only thing the stewardess was capable of saying.

As soon as the stewardess disappeared behind the curtain, everyone started talking. They talked to people they were travelling with, they talked to people left behind by their companions, they talked to people they'd never met before. Over the PA system someone spoke in a language Izumi couldn't recognize. It was apparently one of the hijackers. Then came a female voice shouting what must have been the name of another stewardess. Then came the screams of another woman.

A passenger who understood English jumped up and shouted, "They're saying they can't fly the plane!" The cabin filled with panic, people screaming and wailing.

"We're going to crash!"

"We're going down!"

"No!"

"This can't be happening! We're going to die!"

"You've got to be kidding!"

The middle-aged man sitting next to Izumi suddenly clasped his hands together and began to mumble a stream of words: "*Kuchichuchipa, kuchuchipa, kuchuchikuchikuchichuchipa, kuchukuchuchipakuchikuchikuchikuchi...*" Izumi supposed that the man was speaking in tongues. How had he ended up sitting next to someone like this? How could he come to terms with his own death with that going on next to him?

A stewardess, her hair dishevelled, ran towards the rear of the plane crying, "Mother! Mother!" This, more than anything else, made the hopelessness of the situation clear. People became hysterical. The plane jerked left then right, headed up then down, first like a pendulum, then like a yo-yo.

"Now I understand!" bellowed the man seated in front of Izumi. "Murakami, Maeda. You bastards. You sent me to France so you could take control of the board of directors!"

"Goro! Vera! Who's going to take care of you when I'm gone?" a man cried, holding a photo before him. "Who's going to take care of you?"

"They're just dogs!" said the man next to him.

"I don't care what happens to human beings! You can die, for all I care!"

141

"But there's still so much I wanted to do! I wanted to fuck as many French women as I could! I can't believe it's going to end like this!"

"I was just starting to build my thirteenth miniature! I bought a new cabinet for it, and extra miniature buildings, but now it'll never be finished!"

"*Kuchichuchipa, kuchuchipa, kuchikuchikuchichuchipa, kuchukuchuchipa-kuchikuchikuchikuchikuchi…*"

"Shit! Why did I listen to the health department? We could've just kept selling 'spicy'! We could've made millions! But we had to settle for 'medium'! They couldn't have done anything to us! Then I never would've had to go to France! Shit!"

The lights in the cabin faded to a dark red. Screams filled the air. As his surroundings grew more and more hellish, Izumi felt his fear overcoming him and he stood up, letting out a bellow. Until that point, Izumi had been quietly enduring the chaos, and his sudden change made the man speaking in tongues stop and look up at him. But he soon resumed his chanting, determined not to be outdone by his neighbour.

"*Haramafundaramahanda, fundafundahandarama*

142

handafunda, handa, handarakefundarake, funfunhand-
arafundarahandarama, fundarumafundaruma..."

"They all treated me like Yumiko's lover, even though we only made love three times. But that was enough for me. It was enough. The pink lips of her pussy were so perfect. Those little pink petals. It was paradise. So wet. So wet. If only I could bury my face between her breasts one more time!"

A company president, realizing this was his last chance to reveal his true feelings, turned to his vice-president and embraced him. "I love you. I want you!"

"Sir! I'm sorry! I just can't!" cried the vice-president. "Please just let me die with dignity!"

"Am I that repulsive?" yelled the president, starting to choke the other man.

A stewardess, naked from the waist down, stumbled down the aisle in a frenzy of lust. She clung to the chest of a muscular man and pleaded sultrily, "Let's do it! Please, fuck me!"

"You idiot! You think I can get it up at a time like this?" said the man, pushing the stewardess away.

"I turned everybody down, and now I'm thirty-two and I've never done anything," the stewardess sobbed in the aisle.

A man at the rear of the plane began to dance and sing:

> All my life, I worked myself sick.
> So when I finally got some money, I left on a trip.
> The journey of a lifetime, that's what they said.
> But if the plane crashes, I'm going to Hell instead!

Izumi pushed the babbling man aside to look out the window. What he saw was not the ground, but rather the slanting horizon where the sea met the sky. The creaking body of the plane was heading straight down into the water. Izumi couldn't bear it any longer. He screamed and stumbled out into the aisle. Stewardesses and passengers were embracing one another, crying and yelling that they were going to die, they were going to die!

Izumi was repulsed, but in the next moment decided to join them. He yanked off his pants before climbing on top of the sobbing stewardess in the aisle. He told her he would make love to her, and she begged him to do it quickly, quickly. The entire cabin was an ear-shattering pandemonium of screaming and raving.

"Damn that Murakami! Damn that Maeda! They think they can take over the board when I'm dead! I'll come back and haunt them!"

"Oh, Goro and my dear little Vera! If I die, no one will love you the way I do! I don't want to die! Please, take these other people, but not me! Not me!"

"I wish I'd never gone to France. Those damn French women never really liked me. They never had any problem taking my money, but they laughed behind my back. I worked hard for that money! So hard… It's not fair! It's not fair!"

"I made twelve miniatures and now there'll never be any more! Oh, my precious miniatures! I can see the sea coming up to meet us! It's so empty! Just like my last drawer! We're going to fall into the ocean, and it'll be all over!"

"*Haramafundaramahandara, fundarafundarahandarama, handarafundarahandarake, funfunhandarafundarake, fundarahondarafundarama …*"

"Ha ha ha! I went and made it 'medium' just because the board of health told me to! How could I have been so stupid? That warning was bullshit! I should've just ignored it! If I had known I was going to die, I would've done whatever the hell I wanted! If I had kept it 'spicy', my family would've been set for life! They could've lived in the lap of luxury! Damn it, damn it! And because I went to France to expand our business, I'm going to end up dead! Perfect! Ha ha ha!"

"But if the plane crashes, I'm going to Hell instead!"

"Let's do it! Come on, let's do it!"

"Sir! I just can't do that!"

"I turned everybody down, and now I'm thirty-two and I've never done anything."

"The pink lips of her pussy. Those little pink petals. They were perfect. It was paradise. So wet. So wet. If only I could bury my face between her breasts and come come come one more time!"

There was a bright flash and a burning smell, and the next thing Izumi knew, he was back in his seat. He looked dumbly around him as if he had just woken up. He felt strangely calm. The cabin was dry and cool, and the tranquillity surrounding him made the frenzy of moments before seem like a dream. No, that madness and confusion had been real, Izumi told himself. He looked around to see the other passengers also sitting in their original seats, each with a peaceful expression on his face.

Izumi did his best to analyse his own feelings. Where had this sudden calmness and resignation come from? Where were they? He couldn't see any of the stewardesses – they must have gone back to their stations. And there was no sign of the few non-Japanese who had been on board. What could have happened to them? And how had the plane escaped what seemed like certain destruction? They should have already crashed into the ocean.

Then he understood.

They were dead – all of them. The plane was no longer a part of the real world. They were flying to the world of the dead. Of course. The sudden serenity in the cabin made sense. It was death that had brought about this resignation, this feeling of release from the affairs of the real world, this tranquillity that came from being freed from all worldly desires. He was dead and the only thing left was his immortal form – his spirit. He was really dead. This realization caused him no sadness. The chaos of moments before, and indeed his entire life, seemed like something that had happened to someone else. It was almost funny. Why had he felt such strong feelings of attachment to his life? Why had he dreaded the other side so much?

No, he thought to himself. Now the world of the living was "the other side". *This* was his world now. But where exactly was he? Could this be the "Hell" that everyone talked about? No wonder the non-Japanese had disappeared. They had each gone to their own version of the afterlife.

The man who had been speaking in tongues now sat quietly with his eyes closed.

"Can you see anything out the window?" Izumi asked him.

The man opened his eyes and looked at Izumi before turning to peer out the window. He moved his eyes slowly up and down before speaking in a flat, unemotional voice. "There are no clouds in the sky, but there's mist everywhere. I can't see anything on the ground. It's a flat yellowish brown." He then sat back in his seat and closed his eyes once again.

The plane kept flying smoothly, although Izumi could not imagine who was piloting it. He couldn't hear the sound of the engines. After a while, the plane seemed to descend. He half-expected to hear an announcement come over the PA system, but there was nothing. After a sudden soft jolt, they were on the ground. Izumi hadn't been wearing his seat belt, so he stood up and stretched while the plane taxied to its destination.

"I guess that means we're here," said a man who looked like an executive. He had been sitting three rows ahead of Izumi, and now stood up, nodding and smiling to Izumi. The passengers talked to one another amiably – dying together seemed to bring them close to one another. They acted almost like family members or close friends.

A young man who looked like an engineer walked up to Izumi. "It looks like there's an air-port terminal over there," he said. "I don't see any people though."

Even after the plane had stopped taxiing, most of the passengers remained in their seats, dozing or fidgeting.

"Let's get off," said Izumi. He gathered his carry-on bags and, following the other two men, made for the exit.

The door of the plane was open, and when he stepped outdoors, Izumi was enshrouded by mist. There was no wind, and the air was stagnant and warm. Izumi walked down the steps to the runway and looked around. There was no sign of human life anywhere. Who could have lowered the steps? The terminal was a plain, sterile building, marked only by a neon sign that read "HELL". It glowed crimson even in the middle of the day. Of course, thought Izumi. This wasn't the real world. Anything could happen. The three men walked to the terminal.

"I used to run a food-processing company," said the middle-aged man who had been cursing the board of health minutes before. "For years we made instant soups. Then last year we came up with a line of spicy 'lunch soups'. First we came out with 'mild'. It had a hint of consommé to it. It wasn't very spicy at all. Now, as you know, hot pepper can be addictive. So the next thing we knew, our 'mild' soup was selling quite well. Then we came out with 'medium'. You might not guess it from the name, but 'medium' was actually pretty spicy. That sold even better than 'mild', so we decided to release a 'spicy' version. Now that was really hot. We came out with it six months ago, and it was a huge hit. People all over the country loved it. They couldn't live without it.

"Finally, some young people started complaining that their throats hurt because they were eating too much of it, and the board of health gave us a warning. So we stopped making it and switched back to 'medium'. But it didn't sell at all. Once people tasted the spicy stuff, they just couldn't go back. My company was on the brink of bankruptcy, so I went to France to see if we couldn't sell it there. Then this happened on the way home. Just my luck, huh?" He paused and chuckled. "But now that I'm dead, I couldn't care less about any of it. Actually, I can't believe I spent so much of my life making such ridiculous products."

"I ran an architectural firm," said the young man who looked like an engineer. He was the one who had been screaming about the twelve miniatures. "We mainly designed apartments. It was my dream to design a hundred apartment buildings in a hundred cities across Japan, and I had finished twelve of them. I was so proud of them that I made a miniature of each city with my apartment building right in the middle. I put each of the miniatures in a drawer and whenever I had guests over I would show them off. Then one day I opened the thirteenth drawer – the one that should have been empty – and I saw the sea. I don't know if it was a hallucination, but I was so surprised I slammed the drawer shut. Maybe it was a sign." When the young man had finished talking, he smiled cheerfully and waved his hand as if to dispel any misconceptions the other men might have had. "But now I realize how meaningless that all was. I was like a child, naive and selfish. I always had to have my own way. I guess it's no surprise that I ended up here."

The three men entered the terminal while Izumi was telling his own story. The building was nearly empty. There were no demons waiting to meet them

– not even an immigration checkpoint. A few people who looked like airport employees stood about, but that was all. There was no sign of other travellers in the cavernous lobby area, and there were no duty-free shops or restaurants.

"Visit HELL – where you never need a passport," said Izumi. The three men laughed loudly and proceeded to walk towards the exit.

Izumi stepped onto a city street surrounded by tall office buildings. His two companions had disappeared from his side. The pedestrians and the cars in the street looked exactly as they did in the real world. There was nothing about them that suggested that they were anywhere else. Izumi conjured up the faces of people who had died before him. If he was really in Hell, he might be able to meet some of them again. He began to walk slowly along the pavement.

The lift doors opened, and before Mayumi Shibata and Yoshio Torikai could press the button to shut them again, the buck-toothed reporter and his photographer forced their way in.

"Get out of here!" Torikai screamed.

But the reporter just shook his head and laughed, "We're just a coupla *morons*. You can't expect us to understand you." He ordered the other man to hurry up and take some pictures. The photographer pushed Torikai out of the way and began to shoot close-ups of the horrified Shibata.

"No! No! Stop!" she screamed.

"Stop it!" cried Torikai, trying to push the photographer away.

The reporter tried to pull Torikai off, and in the tussle all four fell to the floor of the lift as the doors closed. The lift began to ascend, perhaps called by someone on a higher floor. Thirty-five... thirty-six... Inside the lift, the struggle continued.

"You think because you're a so-called novelist, you can treat the press like shit? You'll be sorry when my article comes out! Just wait! You'll regret this!"

"I'm not scared of some little piece-of-shit peeping Tom! The literary press will protect me! I'll be the one writing about *you*! You'll never work in this town again!"

"I can't believe a pretty young thing like this

would screw an old geezer like you. In fact, the idea of it makes me sick. But I've got the proof right here on film! The tabloids are gonna eat this up! Your marriage is over, and don't think your little friend here won't leave you when the shit hits the fan!"

"Please," screamed Shibata, "my career will be ruined! I'll do anything! Just stop!" Half-crazed, she began punching the lift buttons at random, causing the lift to come to a bouncing halt as a piercing alarm went off. The lift went dark and yellow emergency lights started blinking.

"Stop it! What the hell are you doing?" yelled the reporter.

"We're gonna fall!" cried the photographer.

"What difference does it make if we fall?" Shibata screamed. "I don't care if I die! I'll take you all with me! Ha ha ha ha!" Her maniacal laughter was enough to send shivers down the spines of the men.

"Settle down, Mayumi," Torikai said, trying to calm her.

"Yeah, just stop it!"

The alarm stopped ringing, but immediately the lift began to shake. Then suddenly it fell. Mayumi

155

screamed and clung onto Torikai. Then the lift jerked to a halt. The control display still read "30", but the lift continued to shake as if it would fall at any moment.

"What do I have waiting for me at home?" cried the photographer. "A wife like Godzilla and three snot-nosed kids! I'm sick of being a slave! Capitalism, the media – it all can go straight to Hell! Let the lift fall, and get it over with! I don't have any reason to live! But if I have to die, I wanna screw a nice piece of tail like this, just once!" He lunged at Shibata, who clawed at his face.

"This is a nightmare!" Shibata started screeching again. "I just bought a double bed and ordered a dress from Chanel! I can't die! A body like this doesn't come cheap! I went to the best spas and hairdressers and had all that expensive plastic surgery, and for what? Get your hands off of me, you sweaty middle-aged lump of shit! You make me want to vomit!"

Meanwhile, the reporter and Torikai had their hands around each other's necks.

"I can't die like this! Now I'll never be the next

Shugoro Yamamoto! I was going to be the king of Japanese literature! I was going to sleep with all the actresses I wanted! I can't die with scum like this!"

"Give me a break, you phoney! You just like the *idea* of being a novelist! The king of Japanese literature? Ha! I bet I got better grades than you at school! I don't care if we die! With teeth like this, I'm screwed for life. But at least they're good enough to bite your ear off, you son of a bitch!"

"You weasel! You spend your time digging up dirt on people. I bet you get off on causing trouble for young women like this. Does it get you all excited? This is probably the closest you'll get to a woman without paying for it!"

With a shower of sparks, the lift began to fall again, but thudded to a halt just as its four occupants had begun to scream. They writhed in the darkness like zombies at the bottom of a grave. What floor were they on? They couldn't tell. Panicked, their hearts in their throats, they felt a queer mixture of love and hate for one another.

"Are we dead yet, Mother?"

"No! No! No! Get this beast off me!"

"Smile! Smile, Maupassant!"

"Pompous fraud!"

"My parents warned me about bourgeois types like you!"

"Come on, you little tramp!"

"Is this the end?"

"Oh Amida, oh Kannon, oh Jesus!"

"Amen! Miso ramen!"

"The *bon* dance at dusk…"

"When will the purple lotus bloom?"

"I feel such loss…"

"Get away from me! You're swarming with germs, you prick!"

"But if I die…"

"Will my memories of her disappear?"

"I was always there to get my story."

"The lion sleeps tonight."

"Who will remember me?"

"Is this the line between life and death?"

"I wish something would happen. This wait is killing me!"

"I think I can see stars."

"There's a dog walking by the side of the river."

"I've waited so long, my dick's swollen like a blowfish!"

"Someone'll come sooner or later."

"No, no! I can't stand this much longer!"

"Can you pry the doors open?"

"It's no good! I can't get any leverage with my fingers!"

"Why don't you try hitting it?"

"No, don't hit it! Don't hit it!"

"The shock could make the whole thing fall!"

"It doesn't seem like anybody's out there!"

"Is anyone there?"

Finally the reporter, desperate, punched the doors, and the lift started to fall once again, accelerating until a deafening roar surrounded them.

"No! Stop it!"

"Here it comes!"

"It's bye-bye blackbird!"

"I believe in the three treasures of Buddha and the grace of Amida!"

"We're going to die!"

Just then the lights came on, illuminating the

fear-contorted faces of the four people huddled in the corners of the lift. The lift had stopped falling.

"What happened? Why have we stopped?"

"Are we on the bottom?"

"It seemed like we were falling for ever!"

"Oh my God. Look at that," said Shibata, pointing to the control display.

Everyone looked up silently. It read "666".

"Oh, come on! There can't be six hundred sixty-six floors to this building! The shock of the fall must've caused the display to malfunction. That's all it is."

"Come on, let's get this door open."

"No, don't. I know it's Hell," said Shibata.

The three men took turns telling Shibata not to be silly. Again they tried to pry the doors open with their fingers, but succeeded only in scratching uselessly at the metal. The doors wouldn't move. Dazed and silent, the four of them looked at each other.

At last Torikai groaned, his voice sounding like it was being squeezed out of his throat. "I think we're dead," he said.

The photographer sighed loudly. "You think so too?" he said without expression. "All my desires, everything I cared about. They're all gone. I don't feel anything. That's proof to me I'm dead."

"You're right. I feel the same way," the reporter nodded.

"What are you all talking about?" said Shibata. "I'm alive. I've got plenty of desires. There're still lots of things that I want to do."

The three men looked at one another.

"*Women!*" they exclaimed in unison.

"Even in death, they can't let go."

"They cling to the vanities of life."

"It's sad, really."

"The persistence of a woman."

The three men laughed nihilistically.

"But isn't that proof that I'm alive? You're the ones who're dead. I am alive!"

Shibata stamped angrily on the floor of the lift, and the doors opened smoothly and silently. It was the lobby of the hotel, looking no different from before. The guests walking back and forth. The hotel staff. The classical music. It was as peaceful as ever. No one seemed to realize that the lift had malfunctioned. The four people in the lift shuffled out into the lobby. Were they alive or dead? They had no idea. They went their separate ways as if trying to take back their lives.

By the age of eighty-five, Nobuteru had grown quite senile.

"Well, if it isn't Takeshi. Welcome, welcome. How is your leg? Any better?" he would say to his brother-in-law Koichi when he came to visit. "You look wonderful," he would say with tears in his eyes. He called his daughter-in-law "Nobuko" and treated her as if she were his wife. His own wife he didn't recognize at all. "Who are you?" he would say whenever he saw her. And when he saw his great-grandson the primary-school student, he would shout, "Yuzo!" and try to hug him.

"Takeshi? Yuzo? Who is he talking about? Do you know, Mother?" asked his son.

"I have no idea." She guessed that they must be some old friends of her husband's, but whenever she asked him about his childhood, he would turn suddenly cross.

"What could have happened back then?"

"I don't know. But something happened, that's for sure."

Nobuteru was too far gone by then for them to find out the truth.

"My father comes from a generation where just about anything was possible," his son Shinichiro would tell people. "Just after the war, it was difficult to tell right from wrong. In fact, you couldn't survive without doing some things that were wrong. Anyway, laws weren't as strict as they are today, so you were more or less free to do what you wanted. You didn't have to worry about environmental problems, and people weren't so concerned about how much education you had. I've even heard people say that when someone swindled you, it was your fault you got swindled. So I guess my father just came up with his own morality. It was the only thing he had to go by. But now he's senile and starting to lose it. He's reverting to his childhood, before he had a sense of right and wrong. So you can never tell what he's going to do. Recently he started wandering away from the house. My mother should really be more careful…"

* * *

It was nice day. Maybe Nobuteru would go out for a walk. Who was this old woman? One of the neighbours' maids? What was she saying? Don't leave the house? He'd go if he wanted to. She had no right to tell him what to do. Now, where were his sandals? And where had Nobuko gone? He hadn't seen much of her recently. Had it been ten years ago that they had got married? No, it was five – maybe two. It didn't matter. The important thing was that she was young and beautiful. She was a good wife. He was proud of her. Where had she gone? She wasn't dead, was she? These days whenever he mentioned a name, someone would say they died long ago. Were all of his friends dead? How sad.

Where was he? How had he ended up here? Who was that walking by? Had he eaten lunch? No, maybe it was breakfast. That pasta sure was tasty. Wait, pasta for breakfast? Must have been lunch after all. Yes, it was lunch. Ha! He wasn't senile after all. Wait a minute. He had the pasta the day before. At a restaurant. What was it called?

The Inferno? Yes, the Inferno Italian Restaurant. He had gone there with Nobuko. Where was she, anyway?

Wait a minute! He knew that old woman. He knew who she was. It was his mother. She had got a lot older, but she was his mother, no question about it. How had she lived so long? How had she lived so long? How had he... lasted so long without eating? He was starving. Starving. His stomach was rumbling. It was like this during the war. Things were tough then. Whatever happened to Takeshi? And what about Yuzo? Were they in school?

Oh, look, children on their way home from school. This road leads to the primary school. The neighbourhood has changed a lot, but this road is the same. Just walk straight along and you reach the primary school. Yes, there's the front gate of the school. There's no school today, so no kids playing in the schoolyard, but there's the raised platform in the middle of it. Wait, there are some boys playing there after all. It's Takeshi and Yuzo! Yes, it's definitely Takeshi and Yuzo. Just as he remembered them. Yuzo as dirty as ever, and Takeshi young and handsome. Hey! Hey! Nobuteru waved to them, and they waved and called back to him.

"You took so long to come that we decided to come and see you ourselves."

"We're just like we used to be, but you've got so old."

"You mean you remember me?"

"What're you talking about? You think we could forget good old Nobuteru? Don't be stupid!"

Nobuteru hugged the two of them and began to sob like a child. Takeshi and Yuzo patted the old man on the back – a gesture that seemed strangely at odds with their childlike appearance.

"We know. You've been thinking about us all this time."

"We died a long time ago, but don't worry. We're not angry about you living so much longer than us."

Nobuko had gone out looking for her husband and found him standing on top of the platform in the schoolyard crying and laughing to himself. She called out to him, thinking that he might finally have gone mad. At the sound of her voice, he quickly returned to his usual self.

"I'm sorry for worrying you, Mother. I'll go home now." He obediently climbed down from the platform. He had mistaken his wife for his mother many times before. She gently put her arm around his waist and led him back home.

Daté and Yuzo were watching a movie. There must have been other people there in the old, dingy theatre – they could make out motion in the darkness. The flickering black-and-white images that the rattling projector created on-screen were of a small room in a run-down part of town – a club, maybe a bar. A meaty, unattractive woman grasped a kitchen knife tightly as she glared down at a man. It was Hattori! He was tied to a chair and looked exhausted. Next to them were three Ikaruga gang members lying on a sofa. They looked exhausted too, and were just watching as the woman did as she wanted with Hattori.

"Let's help him out," Daté whispered to Yuzo, who nodded.

"Just wait a bit longer."

On the screen, Hattori raised his sweat-and-blood-stained face slightly and smiled an eerie smile. "I don't think we're in Kansas any more… We've gone to the other side. And I've taken you all with me."

The *mama-san*, who until that moment had been beating and screaming at Hattori, suddenly stopped. "I'm sorry for using you," she said, "but it helped me work out my hatred of men. It's all gone now. So I don't mind going with you. I can't stand another day of the anger and hatred of the real world." A gentleness came over her as she looked at Hattori.

Her change of heart brought one of the yakuza slowly to his feet. He glared blackly at them. "What do you mean you're taking us with you? You little shit. You think we're just going to let you die? You're just going to Hell anyway, so what's your hurry? Why not stay and enjoy the Hell we have for you right here?"

"Isn't this ever going to end?" Hattori bowed his head and slumped his shoulders. "I'd rather be dead than face any more of this. Please, somebody help me!"

"Who's going to help you?" said the yakuza who was the leader of the three; it was he who had stabbed Yuzo. "This is your Hell. You're never getting out of here. We could keep this up for ever."

On-screen there was a close-up of Hattori's despondent face. In the background, the song 'Nightmare' reached a crescendo, just as the words "THE END" appeared.

"Let's go." Yuzo stood up and began to walk down the aisle.

"We can't let it end like this," said Daté angrily.

The two of them jumped up onto the low stage at the front of the theatre, pushed aside "THE END", and walked into the screen. Yuzo went first, then Daté.

"Hattori! We're here!"

"You think you can do this to our friend and get away with it?"

The three Ikaruga yakuza froze. "Where the hell did you come from?" cried one of them.

"Hey, didn't I just kill you?" asked the leader.

"That's right, and I went to Hell. Then I went into a dream and stepped into a movie and now here I am. Simple." Yuzo snatched the knife from the *mama-san*. "Let's get this over with. Come on, where's the knife you stabbed me with?"

Asahina replied shakily, "I told my man to get rid of the knife along with your body. Come on, can't we talk this over? I can't fight you – you're already dead. You can't kill me, and I can't kill you. Look, your man there is half gone. Whether he pulls through or he goes to Hell with you is your decision. Take him wherever you like. We won't do anything to stop you. We'll just let him go, okay?"

Yuzo laughed loudly. "You want to talk? There's nothing to talk about. Hattori, your lady friend, you and your men – you're all going to Hell with me. In fact, look around. You're already there."

The bar had disappeared. They were standing in a sprawling field, dotted with flickering wisps of flame. They were completely naked. But Yuzo was dressed in a smart-looking suit.

"Now you have to choose an eternal form," he said. "You can be anything – a pig, a dog, a weasel. Take your pick."

* * *

Dreams can show us where our past will take us. They can symbolize our relationships with other people. And they can even predict our fates, showing us clearly and concretely when and how we will die, and beyond.

The Night Walker was stuck between reality and the world of dreams. The living and the dead mingled there, their forms visible in the darkness like anchored boats floating on a sea of shadows.

"Here we are again," said Kashiwazaki, looking around him. "How many times have I had this dream? Or is it the first time and it just feels like I've had it over and over? Look, there's Konzo. And Yumiko and Izumi. Shibata and Nishizawa. Even Osanai is here. If this was real, you couldn't all be here like this. We're not even sure if Konzo is alive or dead, and we heard that Izumi was killed in that place crash. And Osanai certainly has no business being here."

"This is *my* dream," insisted Shibata. "After all, I'm here saying that, aren't I? There can't be any other explanation."

"Well, I certainly wouldn't be in a place like this

if it wasn't a dream," said Nishizawa, irritated. He downed his glass of bourbon. "I can't seem to catch a break at home or at work. I got demoted and still my wife won't stop spending money."

"Of course it's a dream. How else could we all be here?" Osanai was bowing to Kashiwazaki, a pained look on his face as he tried to apologize. "I know I couldn't show my face here otherwise. Not after what I've done."

"Then we must all be having the same dream. But is that really possible?" Yumiko looked around fearfully. She looked away from Izumi as his eyes met hers. "You're a ghost, aren't you?"

"You all know me, so I can be in any of your dreams," said Izumi. He looked calmly at the other people around him. "That's the only way the dead can return to the world of the living."

"Konzo. Konzo. What happened to you?" asked Kashiwazaki, fighting back his tears as he tugged at Konzo's sleeve. "Are you still down under the stage? Are you still alive? Or did you die?"

"It makes no difference if I'm alive or dead. This world and the next are bound together like strands of braided cord." Konzo slowly rose to his feet, walked out to the middle of the empty dance floor and began to dance. "The false death of dreams. The real death of the afterlife. Hell and the world of the living. They're all connected." Konzo assumed a classic kabuki pose. "And now my friends, we must be going. Allow me to be your guide. No, on second thought you have no need of a guide. After all, you have been there before. Leave all your cares and worries behind and follow me to Hell. Allow its cleansing flames to burn away all of your desires, all of your anger. Come. Come."

At Konzo's beckoning, the group left their seats and followed quietly behind him, their expressions blank.

Takeshi, Yuzo and Izumi were sitting at the end of a long conference table. They were on the tenth floor of a high-rise building, in a meeting room that could have accommodated twenty people. Sunlight was streaming in through a large window that overlooked the city street below. The sunlight in Hell looked exactly like sunlight in the real world.

173

"What're you asking me for? How am I supposed to know who's in charge here?" said Takeshi to Izumi with a laugh.

"Well, they have to have some kind of administration, don't they?" said Izumi earnestly. "You have to have some kind of system in place for managing things, even in Hell."

"What do you think?" Takeshi asked Yuzo. He walked over to the window. "If they do have some kind of command centre, where would it be? I guess it could even be in this building right here, for all we know," he joked.

Yuzo walked over next to Takeshi and looked down at the street below.

"Actually, there's something about this place that bothers me too. If I was my old self, I'd probably go find the people in charge and beat the shit out of them."

"If you're serious, I'll help you," said Izumi earnestly. He was still seated at the table. "It's got to be a huge office, filled with computers. There must be dozens, maybe hundreds of people there. If we started trouble, it'd be total madness. It would be interesting. But where is it?"

"It could be in the Devil's Palace," said Takeshi.

"Ah." Izumi grimaced, as if remembering something unpleasant.

"Devil's Palace? What're you two talking about?" Although he would have been bothered by it in life, Yuzo didn't particularly mind that the others knew something he did not..

"Izumi and I just happened to see it a while back when we were out walking."

"It's a place where people go to play a video game called *The Legend of the Devil's Palace*. They're all *otaku* – those guys obsessed with games or movies. We wouldn't have even known about it, but we had a run-in with one of them when we were alive."

"We had just been talking about it when we came upon that building. What was the name of that guy, anyway? He was in sales."

"Yamaguchi. He played that game all the time, even during working hours. Of course, that didn't win him any friends, and I think he just snapped. One day he came to general affairs and demanded the key to the Devil's secret chamber. He was convinced that our building was the Devil's Palace and the president was the Devil. When I tried to talk some sense into him, he slugged me and ran off to the president's office, so I called my boss, Mr Uchida here. His office was on the same floor as the president's."

"I hurried to the president's office to find Yamaguchi strangling the president's secretary, Miss Matsuda. He thought she was a witch. He kept yelling at her to tell him the magic words to open the door to the president's office. I couldn't fight him off – not with my crutches – so I called security and they finally got him under control."

"The president was shocked when he heard about it. And after that, nobody was allowed to play video games on company property." Izumi pointed out the window. "Hey, there it is over there. I wonder if it appeared just now when we were talking about it. You see that gaudy building that looks kind of like a mosque? That's the Devil's Palace. You want to try looking for the control centre there?"

"We don't really need to look for it. If there's an organization running this place, all we have to do is go down there and start some trouble nearby. They'll come to us." Takeshi laughed again. "But I don't think any of us really wants to do that. What's the point? You'll have to admit that you don't have the same desires or curiosity that you had in the real world."

"If Nobuteru was here, he'd think of something interesting to do," said Yuzo, a nostalgic look coming over his face. "But he won't be coming here, will he?"

"No. You can't come here if you're senile," said Takeshi.

"This kind of thing has been bothering me ever since I got here. We all know that senile people can't come to Hell. But *how* do we know it? Who told us? And who decides that they can't come here, anyway?"

"I think maybe *we* do," said Takeshi solemnly. "I think this whole place is a product of all of our subconscious minds. And the whole point of Hell is to get rid of our attachments to our previous lives. Curiosity, hate, love. We're here so we can cleanse ourselves of all of those things."

"And then we can move on." Izumi nodded. "Attain nirvana, or whatever they call it. That's what they've been saying for hundreds of years. Maybe it's created a sort of collective consciousness."

"Who the hell are those guys?" said Yuzo, looking down into the street. "I think they're dancing. And the guy leading them looks like he stepped right out of the Edo period. The other ones don't seem too enthusiastic."

Takeshi also looked out the window. "I think he's a kabuki actor. He's dressed as Iso no Toyata, from that kabuki play. Hey, the guy behind him looks a lot like you, Izumi."

"It seems like you can be in two places at once here." Izumi stood up and walked over to the other two men by the window. He looked down at the group below, unsurprised to see himself walking with them. "That's me, all right. That's a group of regulars from a club called Night Walker. I used to be one of them, so I suppose that's why I'm there."

"What are they doing here?" Yuzo asked Izumi. "Did they all commit suicide together so they could go on a sightseeing tour of Hell or something?"

"I don't know. They could just be dreaming."

"Want to go down there?" A flicker of curiosity

had appeared in Takeshi's eyes. "Don't you want to go meet yourself? I bet that other Izumi would be surprised to see you."

"Could be interesting," Izumi laughed. "Let's go."

"Yeah, come on," said Yuzo. "I think I see some guys from my gang down there too. And the ones with them look like they're from one of the other gangs. It's a regular family reunion."

The three of them slipped through the glass of the window and floated down to the street below.

Sasaki was leisurely drinking an iced tea on a café terrace when he was given a note. He hadn't seen anyone stop by his table, and the waiter certainly hadn't put it there as he passed by. It was as if the note had simply appeared out of thin air.

"Come to the fountain in the square," read the slip of paper. It was written in ballpoint pen.

Sasaki had never been to the square, but somehow he knew exactly where it was. And although no time was mentioned in the note, he felt that he should go immediately. He took a five-hundred-yen coin and three one-hundred-yen coins and placed them on the table before getting up to leave. He didn't know the exact price of the tea, but everything in Hell had a vague, dreamlike quality to it; it really didn't matter how much he paid.

The semicircular fountain was in one corner of the square. Water poured from the open mouths of the demonic faces carved into its stone surface. There was already quite a crowd gathered in front of it. Most of the people there were elderly and many of them seemed to be couples; perhaps they had been married in life. Some wore suits, and others were dressed for hiking. They were divided up into groups of twenty or thirty people standing in two neat rows. A middle-aged woman dressed in a train conductor's uniform appeared and spoke brusquely to Sasaki.

"You'll be your group's leader, Mr Sasaki."

The woman was chubby, dark and unattractive. Her teeth were pointed fangs. How did she know Sasaki's name? Who was she? Was she a demon? He decided that "demon lady" would be as good a name for her as any. She spoke to him again before he could ask what he was supposed to do.

"You're going to lead group seven. The group over at that end is group one, so this is group seven, do you understand? Just stand at the front here and follow group six. If anyone gets out of line or if anything unusual happens, tell me."

Where were they going? How would he tell her if something did happen? How should he address her? And why had he been chosen to be the leader? Sasaki had many questions, but the demon lady looked like she had little patience for such things, so he merely nodded and moved to the front of the line. He turned to his right and saw that his wife was standing at the front of group six.

"Jitsuko," he called.

She looked at him, smiled, and then nodded slowly. "Hello, dear."

"You two were married, I see." The demon lady smiled, showing her fangs. "And you're the youngest ones here. That's why I made you both group leaders." She trotted off towards the front of the first group.

Sasaki stared at Jitsuko. She was wearing the same drab dress she had been wearing on the train, and yet she was beautiful. She had been cute as a young woman, but this was something else. She still looked the same. Her face was as he remembered it, but there was something different about her. It was almost as though she had lived her life free from the hardships that had plagued her for so long. It had been the cold and the hunger that had robbed her of her true beauty. Sasaki really had been responsible for her ugliness. But it seemed ludicrous to try and apologize to her now, so he merely continued to gaze at the beautiful woman who had once been his wife.

There was no obvious signal, but the first group started walking. They left the square and began to snake down a wide avenue nearby. Groups eight and nine were to Sasaki's left, waiting to leave. Where were they going? The advanced age of the group members and the looks of peaceful resignation on their faces seemed to leave only one possibility. Sasaki wasn't sure if they would be "attaining Buddhahood" as people sometimes said, but it seemed clear there was no reason for them to stay in Hell. Did that mean that Sasaki and his wife would be leaving as well? Had they been freed from their worldly desires already? Perhaps that could be said of his wife, but Sasaki hardly felt that he was ready to go. Who decided who would go and who would stay? Was it something that just happened? When you were ready to go, did you just go?

Jitsuko's group began to follow the tail end of the group in front of it. Sasaki also started to walk. He glanced back to see the expressionless faces of the people following him. Reassured, he continued walking.

They were walking down a wide city street lined with tall buildings. After a time they passed through the open entrance of a large building with a domed ceiling that loomed many storeys above them. It was a sort of shopping mall. The central area was surrounded by stores selling food, gifts, musical instruments, clothes, jewellery and the like. There were no pharmacies, but perhaps they were not needed in a world where no one had to worry about getting sick or dying.

The groups came to a stop and lined up just as they had in the square. Sasaki led his own group into position next to group six. He and his wife looked at each other once again, and Jitsuko smiled at him. To Sasaki, it was the most captivating expression imaginable. There was no sign of the demon lady. Maybe she was busy making arrangements for their departure. He was wondering how long they'd waiting there when a delicious aroma wafted by.

"Oh," said Jitsuko, looking up at Sasaki with a distant expression on her face, "they're selling grilled eel."

"It smells good."

"I'll go buy some. We can have it for dinner tonight."

She left her group and disappeared into the crowd of people. Dinner tonight? Where did she think they were going?

"I'll come too," he muttered to himself, walking after her. He felt as if he was being drawn to her.

'Dancing in the Dark' was playing on the sound system of a music store. A number of older couples were dancing to the song in the open area in front of the store. Jitsuko stood watching them.

"May I?" asked Sasaki.

Jitsuko put her hand on his right shoulder, and they began to dance.

They had often gone dancing when they were dating. Dance halls were a Mecca for young lovers; they'd stand packed together in the middle of the dance floor, barely moving as they pressed their bodies up against each another. The last song of the night was always 'Auld Lang Syne', and when it began to play, the lights in the hall would be turned out. Sasaki and Jitsuko never failed to take advantage of the darkness, kissing passionately and sometimes going further.

As they swayed to the strains of 'Dancing in the Dark', Sasaki remembered the times they had groped each other. They could hardly do the same right there in broad daylight, so instead he pressed his right thigh into her crotch as they danced. Jitsuko's eyes glistened. She looked up and let out a wistful sigh. Her face took on a distant expression, and her cheeks were a rosy red. She let out little moans. Was she really feeling something? Didn't that mean that she wasn't yet free of worldly desires? Or was it just a sort of conditioned response brought about by the memory of their time together in the real world?

Out of the corner of his eye, Sasaki saw that the other groups had starting moving. He felt a sudden jolt of panic. What would the demon lady do if they were late?

"Let's go. They're leaving."

Startled, Jitsuko opened her eyes and pulled her body away from him. "You go on ahead," she said.

She disappeared into the crowd again. Did she plan to find a toilet to fix her teary eyes and flushed face? Or did she still want to buy that grilled eel?

When Sasaki returned to his position in front of his group, he was relieved to see that only groups one through three had left. Still, he was worried about whether Jitsuko would return in time to lead group six. He was waiting anxiously for her to come back when group five began to move.

Just then, Jitsuko came running back. Her face had returned to normal and she wasn't carrying anything resembling grilled eel. She approached him and whispered in his ear, "Keep an eye out for the leader of group eight. There's something strange about him."

She hurried back to her position at the head of her

group, and it began to move. Sasaki glanced over at the elderly man standing at the front of group eight. He appeared to be senile. Drool spilt out of his open mouth, and he stared blankly off into the distance. Why had the demon lady made someone like that a group leader? No, even a demon wouldn't have chosen someone in his condition. The man must have been normal while they were in the square and had only turned senile after they had started walking. Maybe the stress of leaving Hell or being chosen as a group leader had been too much for him.

Was it really possible for someone to turn senile after coming to Hell? Sasaki wondered as he followed behind group six. Could that be the fate that awaited all of them when they left Hell? The man might have simply changed earlier than most.

The groups circled the shopping mall and passed through the front entrance onto the street outside. After a while the road started up a gentle incline. Ahead of them was a river spanned by a large bridge. But the groups did not continue across the bridge, instead turning to the left and following a dirt path along the river bank. Sasaki could see the first group in the distance as it walked alongside the river. Now that they were no longer walking in one straight line, he was amazed to see how many people there were.

When Sasaki's group reached the banks of the river, he also turned left and followed the others along the river bank. As he walked, he looked down at the river on his right and periodically glanced back at his group. They all seemed to be there. But wait – the tail end of their procession had broken off. Instead of turning, group eight was following its senile leader straight over the bridge.

If something wasn't done, group nine would follow them as well. He had to report this to the demon lady. But how was he supposed to do that? Everyone in the real world seemed to carry mobile phones, but he didn't have one, and in any case, he didn't know the demon lady's number. He would just have to shout.

"Excuse me! We have a situation here!"

He had barely got the words out of his mouth before the demon lady appeared at his side.

"What is it, Mr Sasaki?"

"Group eight," he said, pointing towards the bridge. The entire group was on the bridge now and its leader was already halfway across.

The demon lady looked at them with a slightly troubled expression, but then shook her head. "It can't be helped. Let them go."

"Really?"

"Yes. It doesn't really matter."

"Group nine is following them too."

"Yes, I see. But it's all right," she said offhandedly. She began to walk briskly towards the front of the line.

Sasaki was a bit put off by her casual attitude, but since she seemed to be in charge, he had no choice but to trust her. Did it really make no difference where the other groups went? Group seven continued walking. They were now the last group in the procession.

They were surrounded now by rice fields, dotted here and there by farmhouses. Sasaki looked left, right, then left again, trying to memorize every detail of the scene. There were clouds in the distance. They seemed to be bubbling up from the ground and looked as though they would swallow the first group as it walked towards them. Was that how they would get to the next world? Did heaven or paradise lie beyond those clouds? Or did nothingness await them? He was curious and a little scared. No matter what happened, he would certainly be changed. But he was already dead. Surely he had nothing to be afraid of. He watched as Jitsuko's group walked into the clouds and vanished.